A JOYFUL BREAK

Dreams of Plain Daughters, Book One

By Diane Craver

DEDICATION

To my loving sister, Carolyn Chavanne,
who always listens to me talk nonstop about life, family,
and my writing.

ACKNOWLEDGMENTS

I want to thank some very special friends. They always are ready to support and encourage me in so many ways. When I first decided to write an Amish romance, these friends were an immense help to me. I bounced story ideas, several covers, and received feedback on several chapters from them. Their comments helped me to write the best book possible. Thank you to Regina Andrews, Stephanie Burkhart, Sue McKlveen, Karen Wiesner, and Celia Yeary.

Also a big thank you to my husband and children for their continued support.

NOTE TO THE READER

The Amish community I've created is fictional, but exists close to Wheat Ridge which is an actual Amish community in the southern part of Ohio where I live. Before I started writing my Amish novel, I did extensive research to portray this wonderful faith as accurately as possible. I've used many rules and traditions common to the Amish way of life. However, there are differences between the various groups and subgroups of Amish communities. This is because the Amish have no central church government; each has its own governing authority. Every local church maintains an individual set of rules, adhering to its own *Ordnung*.

If you live near an Amish community, actions and dialogue in my book may differ from the Amish culture you know.

PENNSYLVANIA DUTCH GLOSSARY

Aenti: aunt

boppli: baby

bopplin: babies

bruder: brother

daed: dad

danki: thank you

Dietsch: Pennsylvania Dutch

dippy: term for easy over eggs

dochdern: daughters

ehemann: husband

eiferich: excited

English/Englischer: not Amish

fraa: wife

freinden: friends

froh: happy

gem gschehre: you're welcome

grandkinner: grandchildren

grossdochdern: granddaughters

gudemariye: good morning

gut: good

in lieb: in love

kaffi: coffee

kapp: prayer covering

kind: child

kinner: children

mamm: mom

naerfich: nervous

onkel: uncle

Ordnung: Set of rules for Amish and Old Order Mennonite living.

rumschpringe: running around; time before an Amish young person officially joined the church, provides a bridge between childhood and adulthood.

schweschder: sister

was iss letz: what's wrong

wunderbaar: wonderful

ya: yes

CHAPTER ONE

Fields Corner, Ohio

Rachel Hershberger took a deep breath, realizing she had to tell her boyfriend, Samuel, what he definitely would not like to hear from her lips. While standing in front of the farm he'd just bought, she thought how it meant one thing. He wanted to make wedding plans, but it was not possible right now. How could she set a date for their wedding when she needed to leave Fields Corner? Before her grandparents and mother died, all she wanted in life was to marry Samuel Weaver and have children.

But things changed when her mother suddenly died at age forty-four. Losing her dear *mamm* had put a huge emptiness in her heart and spirit.

He pulled her next to him. "What do you think? You've been quiet about me buying this land. Do you like it for us?"

She looked into his blue eyes and saw he was eager to hear her opinion. She needed to ease into telling him about her aunt's request. "It's perfect. I love the row of pine trees."

"We can build our house by the tree line. The property's the right size for me. I don't need more than thirty acres. It's enough to raise our own feed for livestock. I'll still have time to help my *daed* with his farming and take furniture orders."

Her wonderful Samuel had everything figured out for their future when she was so unsure now about her life. *I better speak up and tell him about Aunt Carrie's letter.* She fingered her *kapp's* string. "I have something to tell you."

He grinned. "You decided to join the church. You need to hurry talk to Bishop Amos so you can start your classes, and we can get married in November."

She understood what he meant about not waiting any longer to talk to the bishop. Before having an Amish wedding, both needed to be baptized and to become church members. There were usually nine special instruction classes before being allowed to join the church. "I can't join the church yet. I received a letter from Aunt Carrie. She wants me to visit her next week while Violet's on spring break from college."

"Is Adam going to be home too? I could go with you. He invited me to visit sometime."

Samuel had met both of her cousins when they came for her grandparents' funerals. Then two months later, the Robinson family came again for her mother's funeral. Unfortunately, the media got news of her Uncle Scott, the U.S. Senator from Kentucky, attending her mother's, but waited to film until after the ceremony. For both somber occasions, her aunt and uncle left in an Amish buggy to blend in with the rest of the funeral processions. Adam and Samuel enjoyed each other's company even though one was English and other Amish. "Adam isn't going to join us until later at the beach."

He frowned. "What beach?"

"It's such a pretty day. Why don't we sit by the creek to talk?"

"You sound serious. We better get comfortable. I'll grab the Pepsi I brought for us." He left her side to walk to the buggy. She watched him as he bent down to pick up a brown bag. It didn't matter that he was dressed in the usual Amish garb of black pants, dark blue shirt, and suspenders; he looked handsome and special to her. At six foot, he towered over her petite height of five-three. She loved gazing upward at his gentle face.

They held hands while walking toward the creek. "I'm ready to grow a beard and become a husband. You don't have to delay joining the church any longer on my account."

She laughed, remembering a conversation between Samuel and her brother Peter. Both men were the same age, and Samuel had teased married Peter about his beard. He'd said how that was one advantage to being single and not having to let his beard grow. She rubbed his strong chin affectionately. "A wife gets to pull on her husband's beard when he doesn't listen."

"I'll be sure to remember that." He glanced at a log above the creek. "We can sit here and I'll practice listening to you."

She popped open her can and took a sip of the cold drink. "It's *gut*."

"Rachel, you're almost twenty-one and I'm twenty-three. We can't get married until you're baptized and join the church. You need to start instructions soon so we can get married next fall. What's the problem? Violet's spring break should only be for a week."

The traditional ceremony of baptism was held in the fall, so she understood his concern. If she didn't get started soon on her religious education instructions, she wouldn't be allowed to enter the church in the fall. Their wedding would be delayed for a whole year. But it might be anyhow, she thought. "Well, Violet has early finals so it's more like ten days."

"So you'll be gone for longer than a week?"

"Yes." *I'll wait to tell him I might be gone for a month or even longer. Better to build up to it.*

"What does your *daed* think of you leaving?"

"Aunt Carrie wrote my *daed* that she wanted me to visit. He's not *froh* about me going but he gave his permission. He said our year of mourning is over. Aunt Carrie is driving here to get me so I won't have to take the bus to Kentucky." She didn't mention how clever her aunt was in getting her way. She played on her *daed's* sympathy, saying how much she missed her sister Irene and their parents. Aunt Carrie explained in her letter how she wanted her oldest niece to visit, and she knew Irene would want them to spend time together.

Samuel's blue eyes widened. "So you're going to Kentucky, then to the beach. We can go to the beach for our honeymoon. I've always wanted to see the ocean."

Interesting. She didn't recall him ever saying he wanted to go to the beach. "We won't go. Something will happen. Besides few Amish couples go on a honeymoon. We'll be busy cleaning up after the wedding for several days. Judith would kill me if we didn't spend our honeymoon weekend at home to help clean up. And have you forgotten how newlyweds travel to relatives' homes each weekend? That takes months to visit everyone. I guess you've been around too many English folk in your shop and heard about their honeymoons."

"That's true. We don't want to miss out on collecting our wedding gifts. Of course, a lot of these gifts are furniture and quilts. I plan on making all our furniture." He rubbed his chin. "I'd like to go to the beach before my beard gets too long so it'd have to be soon after we marry."

She smiled at him. "Then I can go to the beach again, but right now I need to go before I'm baptized. I want to do my *rumschpringe.*"

He raised his eyebrows in disbelief. "You did your running around with me when you were eighteen. We experienced the English world together then."

She sighed. "I went to one baseball game with you to see the Cincinnati Reds. That was all I did for my *rum-schpringe.*"

"Did you forget Kings Island when I kissed you for the first time?"

"I guess I did." She'd been shocked when he'd kissed her at the amusement park. The Amish stressed to their young people that the courting couple shouldn't have any physical contact. Not even kissing or holding hands. Although it wasn't proper, she'd liked his kiss. She decided to tease him a bit. "Your kiss at the baseball game must have been better. I remember it the best."

He took a big drink of pop. "I bet my kisses would be sweeter on the beach."

"I have to tell you the truth. I've taken care of my siblings for a year since my *mamm* died. I love them but need to take a break and experience different things before I commit to our way of life. I want to feel the sand between my toes and see the blue ocean. And I can't wait to see the dolphins play in the water." She lifted her arm and waved her hand across the rolling fields. "I love our country scenery but at the same time, I'm tired of the green grass and hills. I want to see something different."

He shrugged. "If you look carefully, you see that each blade of grass is a different shade of green."

"But still it's all green."

"I like green. Especially your pretty green eyes."

She gave him a playful nudge. "I'm partial to blue because of your blue eyes. And I already mentioned the ocean and how much I want to see it."

His jaw tightened. *He's going to give me more arguments about leaving.* In a way, she was glad he cared so much about what she did. It was good to know he'd miss her.

He put his can on the ground. After removing his hat, he ran his fingers through wavy brown hair. "It's warm here in the sun. It feels good to have warmer temperatures finally after the cold winter we had. Outer Banks won't be that warm in March."

"We aren't going to their beach house. Aunt Carrie's taking us to a friends' cottage at Cocoa Beach. It'll be warmer in the southern part of the state."

"That's so far. You can't fly. Remember Amish don't use planes."

"Did you forget that Aunt Carrie was Amish before she married..."Her voice broke with irritation. "She knows I won't get on a plane. She's going to drive us to Cocoa Beach."

"What else do you plan on doing on your *rumschpringe*?"

"Not much. Use a computer. Maybe watch movies." *Should I tell Samuel my other reason for visiting? I don't want to hurt him.*

"One reason I bought this particular piece of land was because it's close enough to your *daed's* house. I know how close you're to your family."

"You're a *wunderbaar* man." She squeezed his hand, quickly deciding to share with him her deepest feelings. "I was so close to my *mamm.* Her death is another reason I'm going to visit Aunt Carrie. She's five years older than my mother was, and she has no heart problems. My *mamm* shouldn't have died from a heart attack. She was too young. I wanted her around for many more years. An English doctor would've caught her heart disease. My children will never know their grandmother."

"What are you saying? That your aunt's alive because she's English."

She nodded. "That's what I want to find out. If we had a phone for emergencies, we could've gotten help quicker to my *mamm* and maybe she'd still be alive. And English don't work as hard as we do. *Mamm* worked too hard."

"It was a shock to your *mamm* when your grandparents were killed. That could've had something to do with her death. She died only two months after they did. "

"Why did that teenager have to use his cell phone while driving? He said he didn't see my grandparents' buggy but it was broad daylight." Even though it was the Amish way to forgive people, she couldn't forget the wrong caused by the young driver. He had a responsibility to watch the road and shouldn't have been using his phone.

"It was a terrible tragedy. Your grandparents were an important part of our community." He was quiet for a moment. "Your *mamm* was nineteen when she married your *daed*. You're past that age now. I've been courting you for close to three years."

"That's what worries me. I don't want to follow my *mamm's* path and die when I'm forty-four."

"I don't want you to die in your forties either." He cleared his throat. "How long are you planning on being gone? I can finish my furniture orders before we leave. I only have a dining room table for an English couple that needs to be done soon. Other stuff can wait. That is if it's okay with your Aunt Carrie that I go too."

Her *daed* thought the world of Samuel, but he would never approve of them both going away together when they were not married. Amazing that Samuel would even suggest it. Not a good sign he wanted to go with her. "That's not a good idea. We aren't married. Besides, I might stay with Aunt Carrie for three or four weeks."

He gave her a worried glance. "It sounds like you want a break from me."

"No, not a break from you. Just a break from everything Amish. The time will go fast. You won't have a chance to miss me."

"You've been too isolated and at home all the time with cooking and doing all the housework for your family. Judith should've been more help. Then you could've kept your job at the bakery. My *mamm* misses you and all the customers still ask about you. They want to know when you'll be back. *Mamm* says no one's desserts are as good as yours. Not even hers or Katie's."

Before her mother died, she'd worked in the bakery owned by Mrs. Weaver, Samuel's *mamm*. She loved the Weaver's Bakery filled with sweet smells from all the delicious goods sold to Amish customers as well as to the English tourists. And baking was her passion in the kitchen.

"I do miss talking to the customers. I enjoyed the women talk with your *mamm* and your sister. We laughed and had good times together while working." She sighed. "Judith's talent doesn't seem to be in cooking but I'm hoping it'll improve when I'm away. She's going to grade papers at home and only work at school half a day." Her younger sister, Judith, started teaching the younger Amish students when Miss Miller left the district to get married.

"I hope you get the answers you need and come back here ready to join the church. Once you see Bishop Amos about getting baptized, we can officially become engaged." He drew her into his arms and gave a tender kiss on her mouth. He ran his finger down the side of her cheek. "I'll miss my fair-haired beauty. I don't want you falling in love with some English guy. I don't want to lose you, Rachel. I love you."

"I know. I love you too." *Is my love for Samuel strong enough to marry him,* she wondered. She wanted a marriage like her *mamm* and *daed* had. They were so in love. *But I can't marry Samuel right now with the way I feel about everything.*

* * *

Samuel entered the kitchen, surprised to see his mother still up at nine o'clock. His parents went to bed usually at eight-thirty because they got up at four-thirty each morning. He removed his black felt hat and put it on a wall hook. "Why are you still up?"

She folded a gray dress in front of her. "I finished sewing this for Katie. And I didn't want to wait until morning to hear the good news about my firstborn's wedding details. I know Rachel's *daed* needs to be asked first but I don't see him saying no. Did you and Rachel decide on October or November?"

His *mamm's* face looked so hopeful that he wished his news would be what she wanted to hear. "I'm afraid not. Rachel's not ready to join the church. She's leaving next week to spend time with her Aunt Carrie."

"How much time?"

He shrugged. "I'm not sure. Maybe a few weeks."

She stood and picked up a coffee cup from the table. "I'm surprised she's leaving but it'll be good for Rachel to visit with her aunt. As long as she doesn't stay away too long and can still get baptized this year."

While she spoke to him, he saw his father enter the room.

"What's the rush?" Weaver grabbed his wife around the waist and gave her a kiss. "You were twenty-one when we married. Rachel's not that age yet."

His *mamm* rolled her eyes. "Rachel will be twenty-one next month."

He grinned at his *daed*. "It's a good thing I didn't stay out all night. I didn't realize I'd have both parents waiting on me to get home."

"Samuel, I can make you a sandwich. I have sloppy joes left over."

"Your *mamm* makes the best sloppy joes."

He patted his stomach. "*Danki*, I'd eat a sandwich if I had any room but I'm full. Rachel outdid herself and served meatloaf, mashed potatoes, and green bean casserole. I ate more than my share of her cheese bread."

"I'm sure she had a pie for dessert too. That girl sure can bake." His mother walked to the sink and turned the handle, rinsing her cup.

"She fixed my favorite...butterscotch pie."

"Her family's going to miss her cooking while she's gone." She gave him a concerned glance. "I know you'll miss her too."

He didn't want his parents to think badly of Rachel, but needed to share with them his fear. "She's also leaving Fields Corner to experience a different way of life. I hope she won't be like her Aunt Carrie and decide to become English."

"Carrie would've joined the church if she hadn't met Scott Robinson. She was one of us and was close to her family. But her love for him was stronger than her love for the Plain life." His mother patted his arm. "Rachel will be back. I've seen the way she looks at you."

"*Ya*," his father nodded. "No English man will compare to you, son. Pray and take this time to draw closer to God. And we'll pray for Rachel."

He exhaled a deep breath. *I might as well tell them everything.* "She's upset about her mother's death. She wonders if her mother had been English if she'd still be alive. And she also wants to use this time to experience a few things in the English world."

A worried look passed between his parents which he understood. They realized there was a chance of Rachel not returning to them. She might adopt the English way of life like her Aunt Carrie did. He broke the silence and said, "I wish this Sunday wasn't church day so I could pack a picnic lunch and we could eat by the creek on my property. Rachel's leaving on Monday morning." He'd been working on a picnic table. Maybe he could finish it by Saturday and take it to his new land. They could skip the Sunday supper and singing to have their picnic. Just so the weather stayed warm and didn't suddenly change like it did sometimes in March. In Adams County, weather could drop forty degrees in one day during the spring, changing from sunshine to snowfall in just hours.

"It's good Rachel will attend church before she leaves. I doubt she'll have any Amish church service to attend when she's visiting her Aunt Carrie." His *daed* yawned. "I'm going to bed. It's been a long day." Smiling at Samuel, he continued, "Your *mamm's* the expert on packing picnic lunches."

"I'll be up soon." His mother turned to him. "You should take Rachel on Saturday. Close your store early. Or Katie could take care of the customers for you so you can leave early."

After his mom left the kitchen to join his father, from the window he stared at the sky with all the twinkling stars. He hated to think how this time next week, Rachel would be living in the English world. He should contact Adam and ask him to look out for Rachel. He'd use his business phone in the furniture store. His district allowed phones in businesses for necessary outgoing phone calls, but they were not for socializing. Using a phone to insure Rachel's safety was definitely a necessity with her living away from their Amish community. Although she was almost twenty-one years old, she'd led a sheltered life. Another upsetting thought occurred to him. *I never asked her if her Uncle Scott would be at the beach with them.* If the Senate wasn't in session for spring break, he might join his family in Florida. As a popular senator, the media might try to photograph them while vacationing. That would not be good if the media found out Rachel was with them. For some reason, the English world seemed too fascinated by his Amish faith.

I hope Rachel doesn't become mesmerized by the English. I can't imagine life without her. Am I being punished for being too forward with Rachel? It was unacceptable to kiss, especially before being officially engaged. He'd kissed her already when she was eighteen years old. As members of their community, he was aware of the teaching of Scripture, which said, "Beloved, I urge you as aliens and strangers to abstain from fleshly lusts which wage war against the soul." He wasn't alone in having close physical contact because Peter had shared with him about his dating relationship with Ella. Peter said to him, "After Ella and I knew we were going to get married, we started kissing and petting. I know we shouldn't have, but we never allowed ourselves to go any further. We avoided having premarital sex. That must be saved for the marriage bed."

Before he left the kitchen, he remembered the words from the Bible. "Therefore do not worry about tomorrow, for tomorrow will worry about itself. Each day has enough trouble of its own." (Matthew 6:34). Trust in the Lord was what he needed to do but he'd also do his God given best to make Rachel happy. He could not imagine life without his precious Rachel. Her physical beauty had attracted him in the beginning, but he'd fallen in love with her deeply after he started escorting her home from the Sunday night singing and having conversations at her home. Further dates, when they started going steady meant he got to see her more often. He knew, without a doubt, that he wanted to marry Rachel.

And it didn't hurt he loved her butterscotch pie the best.

CHAPTER TWO

David Hershberger patted his firstborn, Peter, on the back. "Thanks for helping me plow all the fields."

"It felt good to turn the soil. Before you know it, we'll be sowing oats and the seed hay."

He nodded. "I hope Rachel will be home by the time we start planting corn."

"That's in May. I'm sure she'll be home before then."

"I'm not so sure." He removed the harness from Joe, his favorite work horse. "She's eager to leave us. But keeping her here would serve no purpose. She hasn't made any attempt to move on with her life and it's been a year now."

"Samuel's disappointed. He hoped by now that Rachel would be anxious to marry him. He's busy finishing a picnic table so they can enjoy eating outside on his farm before she leaves."

"He's a good Amish man. The kind of man I want my daughter to marry. I never thought she'd put off getting baptized and married." After putting the harness on the hook, he continued, "Remember, how she teased you and Ella. She said she might beat you two lovebirds and have the first wedding in our family. I hope she won't end up like your aunt and marry an English man. I don't want to lose her too. Losing my Irene has left a hole in my heart."

"She'll be back and marry Samuel. Going away from all of us will give her time to think. She'll get things straight in her mind, so she'll be ready to move on with her life. Aunt Carrie respects our Plain life. She won't want to be responsible for Rachel to leave our faith. You don't have to worry about Aunt Carrie. "

He frowned. "There's another reason why Rachel wants to go. She doesn't want to be around me. She blames me for your mother's death. I overheard her tell Judith if we had a phone, maybe her mother wouldn't have died."

"I should've gotten our phone in sooner, but it still might have taken you too long to get to our place." Peter leaned against the stall. "It wasn't your fault the Maddox family went away for a few days."

In the past, they used their English neighbors' phone when it was an emergency. "They wanted to give me a key to their house, but I told them I'd just put their mail and newspaper between the screen door and front door. Rachel also said to Judith how I should've taken your mother to an English doctor. I know Rachel thinks I failed your mother as a husband."

Peter put his arm around him. "*Mamm* complained of being tired. No husband would've taken his wife to a doctor for being tired. We thought her insomnia caused her tiredness. None of us realized she had a heart problem."

His lovely wife had grieved deeply for her parents, so he'd contributed her tiredness to the many sleepless nights she had and depression she felt. Shortly, before her heart attack, Irene complained of numbness in her jaw. *I didn't do right by Irene. I should've taken her to the doctor. I never realized her symptoms meant heart disease. Rachel's right to blame me for Irene's death.* He saw the disappointment in Rachel's eyes when she looked at him. As much as Rachel was hurting, his sadness was great too. He missed Irene and would give anything to have her back with him and their children. He sighed. "I'm going to put a phone shanty in. Or I might put the phone in the barn. I couldn't even think about it until now. It's too late for Irene but if another crisis happens, I don't want to run around trying to get to a pay phone. I want to be able to call for help right away."

"Probably a good idea with the twins. They are more daring than I was at their age. They think of too many things to try. If you decide to build a shanty, I'll help you with it." Peter scooped oats out of the grain bin, dumping the feed in the horses' troughs.

"*Danki.* You're a *gut* son."

"It's our turn to eat a snack. Let's get some of Rachel's delicious pie. Then I better head home." Peter's eyebrows shot up. "Hey, who's cooking when Rachel's gone? Not Judith, I hope."

He grinned at his son. "It's not going to be me or the twins so Judith's the only one left."

"You better see if Grandma Hershberger can make a visit. No man can work eating Judith's food."

"If she stays away too long, I might see if my *mamm* can visit, but Rachel said this will be a good opportunity for Judith to improve her cooking skills before she gets married.

Peter laughed. "Improve what? She can't cook anything."

"It's not entirely her fault. Rachel loves cooking. She took after your dear *mamm* when it comes to cooking delicious food." From the beginning of their marriage, his Irene had been an excellent cook. "Judith has other talents, like teaching and sewing. We'll survive on Judith's meals."

* * *

Rachel glanced at the vinyl-covered floor in the kitchen. The gleaming floor pleased her. She felt satisfaction in seeing a clean kitchen. The light oak cabinets next to the refrigerator and stove with blooming plants on the windowsills made the kitchen cozy. A calendar was on one of the walls. Her *mamm* had loved looking at the pictures of nature for each month of the year. While she was away, the calendar page would change to a new month. What would the month of April bring? Would she still be unsure about her life? On the same wall was a framed

Scripture her *mamm* loved. Silently she read the Bible verses written on the calendar, *I am the light of the world. Whoever follows me will never walk in darkness, but will have the light of life.*

"Did you forget about our cookies?" Matthew asked.

Picking up the plate of cookies from the counter, she said, "Just for a second. You know, Mother loved this time of the day when her children were back home. She enjoyed hearing about the school day." Before picking up the pitcher of milk, she handed more peanut butter cookies to Matthew and Noah.

While replenishing the milk into their glasses, she thought how cute the boys looked. They were seated on backless benches next to their huge table. Blond Matthew had blue eyes while brown-haired Noah had green eyes. They looked like brothers but definitely were not identical twins. Her *mamm* used to say, 'God blessed us with two brown-haired *kinner* and three with blond hair.' Then with a twinkle in his eyes, her *daed* replied, 'We can try for another brown-haired one.' She missed those happy days when the family was complete.

"Will you miss us?" Noah asked, after swallowing a bite.

Funny, how well she knew her brothers. She figured Noah would be the first one to ask about her feelings in leaving. When they first came home from school, she'd told them about her trip. She knew after they absorbed this information and ate a few cookies, both boys would ask questions.

She ruffled Noah's hair. "What do you think? Of course, I will. I love you both a lot. I'll send you a post-card of the beach as soon as I can."

"Who's going to tuck us in at night? We like you coming to our room to listen to how our day went." Matthew gulped a big amount of milk.

If anything could make her want to change the plans to see the ocean, this would be the reason why. *Maybe I should cancel my trip. My little brothers depend on me a lot. I can never replace Mamm but they've responded well to me tucking them in at night and spending quality time with them before they fall asleep.* But deep in her heart, she knew that this trip was necessary for her own survival and healing. "Judith can read to you and tuck you in. That'll be fun to do something different. I might not be gone long at all."

Matthew gave her a puzzled look. "What will you wear when you live with Aunt Carrie? You might have to wear funny clothes, like Violet. *Daed* won't like that."

She wasn't surprised that Matthew asked her about what she'd wear. He was bolder than Noah and the more curious of the two. "Don't worry, Matthew. I'm going to wear my own Plain clothes." Although it might be tempting to shed her own clothes once, wearing something like capris on the beach would help her to feel free. Maybe she could be daring and just for one day borrow Violet's clothes. Wearing a *kapp*, dress, and apron on the beach would draw a lot of attention. She hated it when tourists and the English stared at the Amish.

Noah drank his milk. "But what if you're the only Amish woman?"

"Instead of worrying about what I'll be wearing, I want to talk about what I expect from you two." Staring at her brothers, she said, "You need to mind *Daed* and Judith. Do your chores and your homework. No slacking."

"Who will watch us when we get home from school," Matthew asked. "Judith doesn't leave school until she's cleaned the classrooms."

She felt a twinge of guilt at her selfishness. Judith had her work schedule changed so she could go away. Forty-five students attended their Amish school in Fields Corner. Her mother had been especially proud of Judith becoming a teacher. After graduating from eighth grade, Judith observed the teaching methods of the two Amish teachers. Within a short time, she tried teaching in the two classrooms with the experienced teachers' permission and guidance. When Miss Miller, the teacher of the lower grades left the area to get married; Judith took the position to teach the first four grades. Being an apprentice first gave Judith the confidence she needed to teach her own brothers and the other students.

"Miss Yoder is going to do the school cleaning so Judith can leave early. She'll have her hands full with cooking and laundry while I'm gone." *While I'm gone, Judith might learn to enjoy cooking and housework, so she'll be more helpful in the future,* she thought.

Her brothers moaned at the same time.

"Judith can't cook," Noah said. "We'll starve."

Matthew said in a worried tone, "She'll burn the house down."

"I heard that," Judith said, as she walked into the kitchen. "I only had a small fire."

Rachel remembered coming home from work to a smoke-filled kitchen and a lot of screaming. Judith had decided to fix supper for them one Saturday. Somehow the kitchen counter caught on fire. Although the damage was contained to the counter, she glanced at the white walls, hoping they'd still be white when she returned home.

"I'm sure there won't be any fire happening." She noticed the blush in her sister's cheeks with several strands of blonde hair escaping her black bonnet. "Is it still windy and chilly outside?"

Judith nodded, untying her bonnet. "The calendar might say it's spring but it doesn't feel like it today."

She pointed to the door. "Boys, scoot now. Get your chores done so you'll have some free time to play later. Be sure to wear your jackets."

After they put their rinsed glasses by the sink, Matthew and Noah slid their arms in their jackets and hurried outside.

"Did they behave today in school?"

"*Ya*. They were good." Judith grabbed a cookie. "You make the best cookies. Well, actually everything you fix is delicious. I don't blame Noah for saying that they'll starve when I cook."

She grinned. "They can stand to lose some weight."

"If I see everyone is wasting away, I'll be sure to contact you to come home." Judith opened the refrigerator and grabbed the milk. "We should get through the first few days since you're doing extra baking and cooking on Saturday. Too bad it's not our turn to have church this Sunday. People sometimes leave their food for the hosts."

"But it takes so long to clean up and to put everything away after having a hundred or more people here." She opened the oven door to check her chicken and rice casserole. "I'm glad it's going to be at Weavers. Don't worry. You'll do fine cooking the meals. If you get desperate, toss out some hints to your students to have their mothers send prepared casseroles for you to heat up."

"Rachel, I can't do that. I don't want others to know I can't cook. All Amish women are excellent cooks except me." She sighed. "I'll never get married. Plain men work hard and expect big meals. That's one of their enjoyments in life. It's not like being married to an English husband who works in an office all day instead of doing farm work."

"Well, some English husbands do hard physical work in their careers. Uncle Scott might not eat as much as *Daed* but he likes the usual meat and potatoes. I don't think it matters if we're English or Plain; we enjoy eating. Some Amish women buy from Weaver's Bakery, so you can learn to prepare a few basic meals and buy some prepared food too. Don't worry. You have many wonderful qualities and will make a fine wife. Besides, you're better at sewing than I am. We can swap. When we both are married, I'll cook for you sometimes while you sew clothes for me." She watched Judith take a bite of cookie, noticing how pretty her sister was in her blue dress with her big blue eyes. She was surprised that no one had courted her sister, but Judith was shy outside of the classroom. *Too bad Samuel's brother, Jacob, isn't older. I've seen him looking at Judith with interest.*

Judith stopped eating her cookie. "If I don't marry, I can give you a break and watch your children."

She nodded. "The boys love it when you read to them. You change your voice when you read the different characters' dialogue. I don't do that."

Judith took a deep breath. "I love the sweet fragrance in here when you do your baking."

"Cinnamon's the reason for the pleasant smell. I put the spice in the oatmeal cookie dough." She'd made two kinds of cookies that afternoon for them. The boys loved peanut butter cookies while Judith's favorite was oatmeal raisin.

"Rachel, promise me one thing before you leave us."

"It depends on what you want me to promise."

"Promise that you won't fall in love with an English man. *Mamm* always missed her sister and hated it when Carrie moved away from Fields Corner. It'd break my heart if you left our world."

She had no plans to marry someone English, but she did want to feel the ocean breeze on her face and experience new things. But was it wrong to be so happy about leaving her family and Samuel? "I promise I won't."

Judith giggled. "Samuel wouldn't stand for it anyhow. He's so smitten with you that he'd probably organize an

Amish caravan of buggies to get you and convince you to come home."

"You aren't fooling me." She decided to tease Judith. "You want me to behave so you get to visit Aunt Carrie sometime."

"How did you know that's my main reason for lecturing you? You and our cousin, Violet, better be good and not get into any trouble. And you mentioned that Adam will be at the beach. If he brings any guys with him, be careful. Enjoy your change of environment but not too much." Judith stood. "I better get some papers graded before we eat."

She opened the oven door and carefully removed her shoofly pie. *I wonder if Aunt Carrie ever makes shoofly pies for her family.* Tourists seemed to enjoy eating this type of pie when they visited the Weaver's Bakery. *I do miss working in the bakery and seeing Samuel daily. It was fun when he came to eat lunch with me.* She enjoyed hearing about the furniture he was making. Sometimes she took a break from baking and waiting on customers to run to his shop to watch him work. *Working at the bakery was the perfect job for me. But I did the right thing when I quit my job. I needed to take care of everyone after Mamm passed on.*

While Rachel put the pie on a rack to cool, she realized in a short time that she'd be miles away from everything familiar in her life. Funny, her younger sister should be the one warning her about the English. She'd been around them more than Judith with working at the bakery. But she was afraid that waiting on English customers in the bakery was different from associating with them in an informal non-business atmosphere.

She prayed silently, *Dear Lord, Help me to have a safe trip to Kentucky and to Florida. Please give me the peace and answers I need to move on with my life. You're so good to me to make all this happen for me. And help Judith learn how to cook.*

CHAPTER THREE

Lexington, Kentucky

"Don't mention to anyone that my niece is visiting," Carrie said to her husband Scott as she watched him eat his *dippy* eggs. Although she seldom spoke in her Pennsylvania Dutch language, sometimes she used a few of the words interspersed in her regular English conversation. Scott loved to tease her about using the word *dippy* to describe his cooked over easy eggs. "Not even your administrative assistant. I don't want photographers around Rachel."

He nodded. "Mum's the word. I'm glad Rachel's going to visit. It'll be good for her to have a break and have a chance to relax. Rachel and your other relatives work hard all the time."

"Well, you put a lot of hours in serving our country."

He shrugged. "That's different. I love what I do. The only thing I dislike is being away from you while I'm in D.C. during the week."

She smiled at him. "You have something in common then. Plain people love their work. They find great satisfaction in each small thing they do." She noticed his cup was empty so she picked it up. Before pouring his coffee, she glanced around at all the electrical appliances in the kitchen. She saw her Cuisinart coffeemaker with grind and brew feature, microwave, toaster, and blender. "I wonder what she'll think of our home with all the electrical appliances. It's definitely a big difference from an Amish house. Of course, it's not like Rachel isn't familiar with an English home. I'm sure she's been in the Maddox home. Irene was good friends with Mrs. Maddox. They used to visit back and forth."

"The difference is Mrs. Maddox was never Amish, so it wasn't a surprise to Rachel to see electricity used in their neighbors' house."

Scott always cut quickly to the point. That was one of the many reasons he was an excellent senator. Of course, it also helped he was handsome with just a little gray in his brown hair. He had the clean-cut and rugged look that seemed to inspire confidence in the voters. She sighed. "You're right. Rachel might question me how I could be born and raised Amish, but I adapted to a whole new and completely different lifestyle. I never used electricity or had a cell phone. Now, look at me. I have everything technical and I even text. I know she's looking for answers before she decides to join the church. I want what's best for her, and I feel fairly certain it will be for her to stay Amish. Switching to English would be hard for her."

He leaned across the table and patted her arm. "I'm sorry. I know it's never been easy for you. I still feel guilty that you gave up so much to marry me. You left your family and your faith, but I can't imagine you not being in my life. We belong together."

"Even though I'm lousy at giving speeches," she asked. When Scott first ran for political office, she'd begged off giving speeches. She cited her lack of education, which was true. As an Amish student, she'd only completed the customary eighth grade education. However, she'd received her GED before they married. After hearing some nasty comments made by women in Scott's campaign office, she took a few classes at the local community college. They probably realized she was in the back office but maybe not. They'd made fun of her and she remembered the cutting comments, especially made by one woman. *What a hindrance she is to Scott's career. Why would a college educated man marry someone like Carrie... a simple Amish woman with no higher education or skills?*

"That's not true. You speak with sincerity and the audiences like you."

She twirled a long lock of her hair around her finger. "Is that why your campaign manager looks terrified when I get behind the podium?"

Looking amused, Scott said, "He did in the beginning. But he doesn't now because you've done great."

"I guess it's easy to go up when you start at the bottom. My prayer group has been awesome. They pray each time I give a speech. Since I can't be a teacher's assistant any longer, I'm thinking of going to college to become a reading specialist." For a couple of years, she had liked being a teacher's assistant in the elementary grades. When she took off to help Scott with his last campaign, she wasn't able to resume her job. Requirements had changed, and teacher assistants had to have at least two years of college to be hired in the school system.

When their landline phone rang, she left their breakfast nook to answer it. The caller ID showed it was her friend Marlene's husband Greg. It was nice how they were both friends to their next door neighbors. "Honey, it's Greg," she said while handing the receiver to Scott.

"He mentioned playing golf this morning," Scott said, before taking the call.

I should hit the treadmill when Scott goes golfing. One thing about being Plain, you never have to worry about exercising. Physical work was part of daily life so you definitely could eat more. Without electricity in the houses, Amish women burned more calories as they did their household chores.

While Scott talked on the phone, she tidied up the kitchen. Talking about giving speeches to Scott reminded her of reporters. *I hate it when they pester me about being raised Amish.* They seem to enjoy asking the same old questions. Do you regret giving up your Amish faith? Are you shunned by your family? *They want to hear dirty details of being rejected, but fortunately I met Scott before I was baptized and joined the church. Would I have given up my close-knit community of relatives and friends if I'd already been a member?* It would've been even harder because then shunning would've occurred. *I don't think I could have married Scott and risked losing my family.* The questions about her background had died down, but with the deaths of her parents and sister, the whole situation with reporters had flared up again.

The media mustn't find out about Rachel visiting and going to the beach with them. Not only would it be upsetting for her niece, but she hated to think what David would do. She was still surprised that he was allowing Rachel to visit her. Nothing must ruin their time together. She'd promised David that she'd protect Rachel as much as possible from the outside world. *With Scott not going with us, we should be safe.*

And she definitely wouldn't give any speeches at Cocoa Beach.

* * *

Fields Corner, Ohio

"Katie, thanks for changing your party to today so I could attend. The brunch was yummy." Rachel had never been to a Pampered Chef party before, so was glad her friend changed it to Saturday. She bought a deep dish pie plate but nothing else. Maybe later she could purchase a few more things when she had a paying job again.

"It worked out for us to have it today instead of next week. The house was already clean for tomorrow's church service. Samuel's disappointed that the weather changed and you can't have a picnic, but you two lovebirds will have this evening to spend time together."

"And we'll have time tomorrow after church."

"I'm glad everyone's left. I need to talk to you." Katie stopped wiping a dish to look at her. "I need your advice."

Rachel finished washing the last plate before smiling at her friend. "That's a change for me. Everyone keeps giving me advice about visiting Aunt Carrie. My *daed* has given me lots of instructions. Samuel has too. Your mother even did today. What's the problem?"

"Timothy told me that we should put off getting married in November."

"What reason did he give?" *Timothy and I seem to be on the same page about needing more time to think about marriage.*

Katie's blue eyes looked troubled. "He's vague. I'm worried because Samuel saw him talking to an English woman in town. Maybe he doesn't want to marry me now. "

Rachel let the water out of the kitchen sink and squeezed the excess water out of the dishrag. "I'm sure he's not interested in an English woman. She was probably a tourist asking him questions. You know how the English are always full of questions for us. Timothy loves you."

Katie sighed. "I never expected this delay. I thought we both were ready. He just acts different around me now."

"Getting married is a big step." She paused for a moment. "Have you ever wanted to experience something new? And see what else is out there before settling down to married life?"

When Katie shook her head, a lock of brown hair slipped from under her *kapp*. "No, I haven't. I want to get married and have *bopplin*."

She grinned. "I guess I can't talk you into going with me to the beach. I can't wait to feel the rush of seawater on my feet and just gaze at the vastness of the ocean."

"We went once to a lake that had a sandy beach. I didn't like the sand, so going to the beach doesn't sound like fun to me." Katie tucked the stray lock of hair under her *kapp*.

"Well, I'll bring you back seashells anyhow."

"If Timothy and I don't get married in November, then you and Samuel can have November for your wedding. My silly brother mentioned getting married in October just so he could get married first."

"Samuel mentioned November to me."

"What's this about weddings?" Katie's mother asked as she entered the kitchen with a broad smile on her face.

Katie said, "I was just telling Rachel that she could have a November wedding."

"December is a nice month too." Mrs. Weaver's expression softened. "I married your father in December."

"I'm glad you married *Daed* or I wouldn't be here." Katie pulled out a chair. "*Mamm*, rest a bit. Rachel helped me and everything's been washed and put away."

Rachel noticed Mrs. Weaver's face looked tired as she walked slowly to a chair. It was time-consuming getting the house and grounds ready to host church services.

Each church district had approximately one hundred members, so it was a big gathering. When they had it the last time, they spruced up the house by painting all the rooms and cleaning up the yard. *It's a good thing it isn't our turn for a few months. I couldn't leave if it was our turn to host the church services,* she realized.

"I think I will." After Mrs. Weaver sat, she said, "Why don't you two rest, too, and we'll enjoy a cup of coffee."

Rachel nodded. "Sounds good to me."

While Katie poured coffee into three white cups, Mrs. Weaver said, "Talking about weddings reminds me of Irene. Your *mamm's* grandparents moved to Fields Corner when Carrie was thirteen and Irene was eight. Esther and Jonas fit in our community immediately. Irene became my best friend...just like you and Katie." She smiled at both of them before continuing, "Rachel, when your *daed* left his district, he bought land close to Fields Corner. Your *daed's* friend, Amos, moved around the same time. They'd grown up together but their district had reached its limit. So they both decided to move. They didn't want to move too far from their families, though. And, of course, now Amos is our new bishop. It's nice your Grandma and Grandpa Hershberger are close enough to travel by buggy to visit. Your *daed* fell in love with Irene at first glance."

Rachel carried her cup to the table and sat across from Mrs. Weaver. *Had it been a good thing for her mamm?* She wanted to believe it had been, but felt doubt about her mother's husband.

"It must have been fun to be pregnant the same time as your best friend," Katie said.

"You could share a lot about your *kinner*. Especially when you both had such great daughters." Rachel grinned at Mrs. Weaver.

Mrs. Weaver took a sip of coffee before continuing with her reminiscing. "It was fun having *kinner* the same ages. When Irene got pregnant with the twins, I was disappointed that I wasn't."

Rachel laughed. "Some days I'd say it was a blessing. Both Matthew and Noah try our patience at times."

"I think it'd be fun to have twins but a boy and a girl," Katie said.

A sad look crossed Mrs. Weaver's face. "I'm sorry Irene won't see you get married, Rachel. We were both pleased when Samuel started courting you."

Katie raised her eyebrows. "*Pleased*, that's putting it mildly. I was surprised you two didn't throw a big party to celebrate."

"I don't know why she had to die so young." Her *mamm* had been so full of life and love for their family. No wonder her *daed* seemed lost without the love of his life. She wondered if he'd ever move on and get remarried. In some ways, she hoped not. It'd be hard to see another woman trying to fill her mother's shoes.

"It was God's will." Mrs. Weaver squeezed her hand. "Don't stay away too long. I'll miss my future daughter-in-law."

What could she say? She might not marry Samuel. Although she loved him, she just felt doubts about everything. She couldn't believe Timothy was also having reservations about getting married this year. Time would tell what she felt was God's will for her. It might be to marry Samuel or it might not be His will for her life. "Samuel's a *wunderbaar* man. And part of a *gut* family."

* * *

On Saturday night, they ate popcorn and drank home-made grape juice while playing the game, Sequence. When it was her turn, Samuel decided to tell her something. "I called Adam."

"Oh, does Adam want you to make furniture for him again?" Rachel showed one of her cards before placing a chip on a space on the board that matched her card exactly.

"No, it wasn't about furniture. We talked about your visit." He watched Rachel toss her card on the discarded stack.

"What about it?"

"I asked Adam to look out for you. You are so beautiful that I'm afraid a college guy on spring break or someone else might take advantage of you in some way. I don't want to see you hurt."

She looked surprised. "I don't think Cocoa Beach is a top spot for college students to visit during spring break."

"How do you know it isn't?" What was Rachel doing, he wondered. Was she checking out Cocoa Beach to see how much fun she could have during her *rumschpringe*?

"Violet told me it's not a party spot for college students. Obviously, she should know since she's one."

Rachel cleared her throat. "I know you meant well but you shouldn't have called Adam. I'm capable of taking care of myself."

"Some guy might sweet talk you into riding in his car to get ice cream or something."

She straightened her body and glared at him. "Give me some credit for having some sense. I'm not going to hop into a car with a stranger."

Great, now I made Rachel upset with me. Not a good thing right before she leaves on her trip. "You're going somewhere you've never been before, and you told me how you want to experience new things. I love you so I'm concerned about you being somewhere new and outlandish."

"Are you forgetting that I'll also be with Violet and Aunt Carrie?" She frowned. "Would you like to call them too? Maybe Adam can't handle me. I might be too wild for one adult to control."

He should've kept his big mouth shut and not mentioned his call to Adam. "I'm sorry. You're right. I have no reason to worry."

She exhaled a deep breath. "I love you, Samuel. But if I'm old enough to marry you, then I should be old enough to visit my aunt without you calling my cousin to keep track of me." Her green eyes filled with kindness. "But it was thoughtful of you to go to the trouble of using a phone to talk to Adam. I know you felt like it was an emergency."

"Don't forget to write to me."

She nodded. "I'll write you a lot of letters. And if I get in a car with a man, I'll be sure to let you know."

Before exploding at her comment, he noticed the mischievous look in her gaze. Even though he realized she was teasing him, he wasn't reassured. *I need to get off this whole topic of her being in a new environment with new people. Her appearance should be a safe subject.* "You look pretty in your green dress. Is it new?"

Glancing down at her dress, she said, "*Ya.* Judith finished sewing it for me while I did some baking yesterday. Our year of mourning is over so she's been making us new dresses that aren't black. She picked out the fabric and said it made my eyes look greener."

"*Ya*, Judith's right." He knew it was his turn to play, but suddenly he became worried about something Rachel said about writing. "If you plan to write me lots of letters, then it sounds like you are going to be away for a long time."

"I don't know how long, but even if I should stay in Kentucky for a couple of weeks, I'll be writing you a lot."

He grinned at Rachel. "I'd rather you'd be kissing me a lot and be here."

She swallowed what was left of her grape juice. "At least, you don't have to worry about me kissing an English guy on the beach."

"Why's that?" *Please say you only want to kiss me.*

"*Mamm* told me that you should only kiss the guy you'll be marrying." She playfully snapped his suspender. "I've already kissed you so I can't kiss anyone else."

"So you're stuck with me." His heart felt lighter with her mention of marrying him. *Rachel might miss me and return home quickly to start her instructions to join the church. Then we can get married in the fall.*

"That is if I decide to join the church and get married, you'll be my husband."

He placed his fifth chip in his row on the board. Why did she have to add *if* to her statement? He'd have some heavy praying to do in the next few weeks. He hoped it would be God's will for Rachel to marry him. "How about a kiss right now? I already won the game."

CHAPTER FOUR

Rachel glanced around at all the young Amish men and women present for the Sunday sing at Weavers. Some were at or near age sixteen while others were older teens. Several were her age and Samuel's. She felt huge disappointment that Judith stayed home. *Why couldn't Judith, for once leave her comfort zone and attend with me?* Obviously, her sister wasn't interested in anyone from their district, or she'd have started going to these social nights. Or maybe she was interested in someone but too shy to do anything about it. How would her sister find a life partner if she never socialized? Most young adults found their spouse during the Sunday evening gatherings. If she'd been like Judith, Samuel might have another girlfriend now. It was at a Sunday sing that he'd asked to take her home. She remembered being nervous riding the first time with Samuel in his open-topped courting buggy.

Well, they might have become a couple just because their mothers were close friends. Before her mother died, they'd enjoyed spending time with the Weaver family.

She noticed Mary Zook talking with another young woman close to the long tables. She stared at Mary for a moment before turning to Katie. "Maybe Mary will meet someone this evening. There are a lot of people here from other districts." Judith popped into her mind again. *I should've tried harder to convince Judith to stay for the evening singing, but she wanted to go home with their daed and boys.*

"I forgot to tell you yesterday that Mary came to the bakery on Friday," Katie whispered. "She asked when you were leaving."

She grinned at Katie. "Should I warn Samuel? Of course, he might like attention from Mary while I'm away."

"I'm glad you find it amusing. She's always had her eye on my brother. I don't want her for a sister-in-law."

Mrs. Weaver touched Rachel's shoulder. "Are you and Samuel staying for the singing?"

She nodded. "Yes. He went out to feed the livestock."

"Where did Timothy go?" Mrs. Weaver directed her question to Katie.

Katie sighed. "He left after the church meal because he had a few things to do. He didn't say what he had to do and I didn't ask."

Rachel hated seeing Katie's downcast eyes. Was Timothy seeing an English woman instead of spending time with Katie?

"You two better take your seats. Samuel's back." Mrs. Weaver smiled at Rachel. "You don't want a certain young woman to sit across from Samuel."

Rachel felt a flash of irritation that even Mrs. Weaver knew Mary was interested in Samuel. Why didn't Mary find her own young man? She followed Katie to the long table where the boys sat on one side of the long table and the girls sat on the other side. The Weavers had a removable wall which separated the kitchen from the living room in their split style farmhouse. Whenever they hosted the Sunday church service and singing, the wall was removed so a long open space existed. The area seated over a hundred people.

After sitting across from Samuel, he winked at her. "It's been a long time since I saw you. Did you miss me?"

She giggled. "Of course."

* * *

After the singing was over, they went outside to Samuel's buggy. Once she was seated, he threw a small blanket over her knees. "It's a chilly spring night so I brought hot chocolate for us to enjoy."

"Does that mean we aren't going back to my house right away?" Maybe he wanted a few sweet kisses between them. Pleasure went through her body just thinking of Samuel hugging and kissing her.

With a slap of the reins, Samuel set his buggy in motion. "If it's okay with you, I thought we'd go to town."

"I don't know. I hate going there late at night. I'm afraid some driver will hit the buggy with their vehicle. I know you have orange reflectors on the back of the buggy and lights on the top but it still worries me. There are accidents even when there are reflectors on the buggies."

"I understand. I can show you the picnic table some other time."

She touched his arm. "I thought maybe you wanted to go to the store to kiss me."

"That too." He grinned at her. "You know me too well."

"We can drink our hot chocolate at your property. It's on the way to my house." Since they were not going to the furniture store, she knew Samuel would like to stop at his newly purchased land. Pride was a sin but she thought God understand Samuel's sense of accomplishment at buying his piece of property.

"I like that suggestion."

"Katie mentioned you saw Timothy with an English woman. Do you think he might date her instead of Katie?"

His blue eyes met her green ones. "When I saw him with the young woman, they were laughing and talking together. She gave him a hug before she got into her car."

"Poor Katie. She has reason to be concerned about Tim. Did he know you saw him?"

He shook his head. "I was across the street and he never looked my way."

"I hope that's not what changed his mind about waiting to marry Katie. I thought God specifically wanted Katie and Timothy to marry. They seem so right for each other."

"It might still happen."

Before passing the buggy, a driver gave a quick beep. Samuel frowned. "I wish they wouldn't honk. At least, this driver didn't continually honk his horn. When they do, it startles Susie and she rears up."

"That's one thing I don't miss about working at the bakery. Buttercup is usually a good road-safe horse except she does get spooked from fast-moving motor vehicles. And in the mornings, many English drivers are in a hurry to get to work so they would beep their horns and pass my buggy a lot."

"I hope you have a safe trip to Florida. Maybe I'll call Violet's cell phone during your road trip to see how far you are."

"Aunt Carrie's a good driver."

"Is Violet going to drive too?"

"I think so. I don't want Aunt Carrie to have to drive all the way herself."

"Whoa, Susie." Samuel pulled on the reins after they pulled into a wide path on his land. "We won't stay long. The wind is picking up. I don't want you to get too cold."

She smiled. "I can take a little cold weather and wind."

"I don't know. You're so small. The wind might just pick you up and carry you away."

"I'll miss your teasing."

He unscrewed the thermos cup and poured hot chocolate into it. After he handed her the drink, he poured again in a Styrofoam cup.

While sipping their hot beverages, Rachel gazed at the twinkling stars. "The hot chocolate is good. Thank you for bringing it."

"I grabbed some of your cookies when we decided not to stay for snacks. Would you like one?"

"I'm glad we didn't stay after the singing so we could spend time alone before I leave tomorrow."

As he leaned to get a cookie out of a paper bag, his hand brushed against her leg. Warmth shot through her body. "No, *danki*. You can take some of my cookies in your lunch and think of me."

"I'll definitely be thinking about you. I want you to have a good time, but not so much fun that you decide not to come home."

She sipped her drink, enjoying the sweetness of the mixture. "This hot chocolate is as sweet as you." *What would happen if I can't remain Amish? I can't imagine losing Samuel.* "If I don't join the church, what will we do? You're already baptized. I couldn't bear for you to be shunned by your family."

"I'm praying you'll forgive your *daed* and come home to all of us."

"It's not just about forgiveness but how strict the *Ordnung* is. Since my *mamm* passed on, I've been noticing how Amish women look older than their age." She stared into her cup, thinking how Aunt Carrie looked so much younger than her age. "I suppose some of it is because we don't wear makeup like English women, but a lot of it might be because we work hard all day."

"English people don't have it easy. They have a lot of different demands on their time than we do. I think it might be harder for them to stay focused on God. They have many distractions that we don't have to put up with."

"*Ya*, that's true, but their daily distractions don't cause them to have heart attacks at age forty-four, like my *mamm*."

"It was God's will for your *mamm* to die when she did. Even if she'd gotten medical attention in time, she might have still died. We don't know. Your *daed* is grieving too."

"I heard in another Amish district, the bishop gave permission to business owners to have cell phones to use to conduct their business. He said to charge them at the English neighbors' houses. I've thought of getting a cell phone because that way if one of us has a medical emergency, I'll have the means to call to get help instantly." She put the empty thermos cup on the buggy seat.

His eyes narrowed. "I like landline phones better. It's easier to keep the phone separate from the home when there's a phone shanty or a phone in the barn. If teenagers have cell phones, they might be tempted to use them too often. Cell phones invade our Amish home life."

"That's true, but I'd use the cell phone just for emergencies." She grinned. "And I'm not a teenage girl."

"No, you're a beautiful woman." He tossed his cup into a bag and took her hand in his. "I hope you decide to join the church. I can't imagine my life without you in it."

"That's a big concern of mine because if I decide to become English, I'll lose you. I know you can't marry me if

I'm not Amish." *Would Samuel leave his Amish faith if I decide not to accept the rules of the Ordnung? His family and friends would have to shun him if he did. But I can't see him doing this even though, he loves me. Losing Samuel would break my heart, but I can't commit until I experience living in the English world.*

"God will direct your decision. It's good you're taking time to pray about why you can't move on with your life and join the church. I'll admit I'm a bit worried you might decide not to get baptized this spring. I keep thinking how your *aenti* became English."

She hated seeing the worried look on Samuel's face. "I'm sorry I'm difficult. Our situation's not the same as my Aunt Carrie's. She met Scott while living in our world. If she hadn't met him, I'm sure she would've taken instructions and joined our church."

"Exactly. You haven't met an English man who makes you question your way of life."

"Instead, it's an Amish man who causes me to doubt."

"I wish your *daed* had installed a phone in his barn or built a shanty, but if you become my wife, we'll have a phone. I'll take you to an English doctor whenever you're ill. I'll be a *gut* husband."

She squeezed his hand. "I know. You're perfect for me." Had her *mamm* thought her *daed* was perfect before she married him? People changed sometimes during marriage. Maybe in her *daed's* case he had too many responsibilities and couldn't do everything a husband should for his wife. The Amish life was filled with hard work but shouldn't her *daed* have paid more attention to the most important woman in his life?

"Enough talking." He gently embraced her and kissed her with urgency.

When he broke their kiss, she murmured, "I'll miss kissing you."

"Kissing you is the best part of my day."

"You say the nicest things, Samuel."

"Remember that when you're on the beach."

She couldn't resist kidding him a bit. "I'm sure I'll have a few thoughts of you while I'm in Florida."

Susie snorted.

Samuel laughed. "I don't think Susie believes your comment."

CHAPTER FIVE

"*Daed*, I'll write the family." Rachel thought her father's eyes looked moist, but she couldn't honor his request and write to him alone. She'd write a family letter and probably individual ones to her siblings. He was the main reason she felt a need to leave home. How could a loving husband ignore his wife's request to see a doctor? Resentment also existed toward him for assuming she'd take her *mamm's* place. He'd expected her to quit her job at the bakery to take care of their family. He didn't expect as much from Judith, and she knew why. Judith was his favorite daughter. Why couldn't Judith have made any sacrifices after their *mamm* died? She did appreciate her sister helping at home now so she could leave, but still for a whole year, she'd been responsible for the laundry, housework, cooking, garden work, and canning last summer. Well, Judith had taken over all the sewing of new clothes and mending. *That was something, I guess.*

I hope my issues with Daed will be resolved by getting away from him. Her stomach turned just thinking about her father.

It was the first time she'd ever gone on a trip without her family. She'd miss them but felt a sense of freedom and excitement that she'd never felt before in her whole life.

Her father cleared his throat a couple of times. "*Danki*, for baking enough bread for the week and making my favorite cookies."

Aunt Carrie smiled. "When I saw everything Rachel prepared, I thought maybe Judith was coming with us too."

He glanced at the cooler and bags in the car. "With all this food, it looks like you're taking all my *kinner*. Did you leave any food for Weaver's other customers?"

She agreed with her father. Aunt Carrie had bought a lot—pies, bread, noodles and cookies at Weaver's Bakery. Then her *aenti* bought meat and cheese at Yoder's Market to put in her cooler. *Will I ever get a chance to eat English food?* she wondered.

Aunt Carrie's dark blond hair came loose from her bun, and she immediately redid the thick strands back into a neat chignon. "You know I always stock up on Amish food whenever I visit. The bad thing is I eat a lot of it and gain weight, but this time Violet will be home to help us eat some of these goodies. And I'm giving some to the women in my prayer group."

He grinned. "I'm glad you and Rachel aren't eating all of it. Have a safe trip."

"Thanks, David." Aunt Carrie briefly patted his arm. "I'll be sure to see Peter, Judith and the boys when I bring Rachel home. I hope those two nephews of mine behave while Rachel's gone."

"*Ya.* Those two are something." Turning to Rachel, his eyes became serious. "Remember to pray during your visit and stay close to God."

His worn and wrinkled face touched a chord in her. She knew her father worried about her *rumschpringe* in the English world. "I will." In spite of her unhappiness with her father, he did love her. She gave him a quick hug. "Take care of yourself."

"We better get going." Aunt Carrie opened the car door. "I don't want to be late picking up Violet."

"I can't wait to see my cousin." Violet's flight was scheduled to land at four-thirty at the Lexington Airport. Rachel had never been at an airport, so she looked forward to seeing the big jets arrive and take off; she couldn't imagine flying. She'd have to ask Violet what it was like to get on a plane and get some place so quickly. Driving by car was definitely faster than traveling by buggy, but she understood why her people couldn't own cars. Avoiding worldliness and keeping the family close to home was essential to their plain way of life. The temptation to just hop in the car and go to town or farther places would expose them to a fast and glitzy world. *But it's fun to ride in a car occasionally,* she thought.

Before Rachel shut the car door, she overheard Aunt Carrie speak in a lowered voice. "David, don't worry. Everything will be fine."

As Aunt Carrie drove away, her chest felt heavy leaving the only home she'd ever known. Glancing back at the white two-story house she grew up in, Rachel saw her *daed* staring at the car. She waved to him before whirling back around in the seat.

"I can't wait until we get to the beach."

Aunt Carrie grinned at her before turning on the road. "Violet and I adore going to the seashore. I hope you'll like it too."

"Will the beach be private?"

"We'll have a private entrance to the beach, but there are other guests who might be vacationing at their nearby houses. I don't think it'll be crowded since the beach isn't open to the general public. The swimming pool's private, though. Each property has a pool."

She smoothed her light blue dress. "The bishop allowed us girls to wear one-piece swimming suits when we took swimming lessons. I was twelve so my suit doesn't fit now."

Aunt Carrie drove slowly by Samuel's furniture store, which was right next door to Weaver's Bakery. She gave the horn a quick beep. "I told Samuel I'd toot the horn when we went by his furniture store, so he knows his girl's on her way to Kentucky. I'm glad I got to talk to him this morning when I bought my goodies at his mother's bakery. Sweetie, he's definitely into you as Violet and Adam would say. You two make a cute couple."

"*Ya*, he's anxious for me to join the church so we can get married."

Aunt Carrie stopped at the only traffic light in Fields Corner. "I'm glad you decided to take time to think things through before making a commitment. Even though I fell in love with your Uncle Scott soon after we met, I waited a few years to be sure."

Suddenly, she had an urge to see Samuel before leaving Fields Corner. "Aunt Carrie, would you mind pulling over so I can run into Samuel's store? I want to see the picnic table he just finished. I'll hurry. I don't want to make you late to get Violet."

"I'll just turn around so you won't have to walk as far. It's no trouble."

While her aunt drove to the furniture store, she thought, *I can't believe I haven't even left yet, and I already want to say good-bye again to Samuel.*

As soon as the SUV was stopped in front of the store, she opened the door and over her shoulder said, "*Danki,* Aunt Carrie. You're the best."

She hurried inside the store and looked around for Samuel. She found him at his desk. "I just have a minute. I asked Aunt Carrie to stop so I could see the picnic table."

His blue eyes filled with amusement. "You sure it's the table you want to see."

"Why else would I be here? I just saw you last night."

He stood, looking down at her. "I'm glad you're here, even though it's to see the table. It's back of the lawn chairs."

Following Samuel, she glanced at his rocking chairs and other pieces of furniture he had for sale. "Everything you make turns out so well."

"I'm glad God blessed me with the furniture business. I wouldn't want to farm full-time." He stopped by an oval table. "I made it out of poly-wood so it will last forever with care."

She saw four benches next to the table. "The table and benches look great. The dark green you used on the legs is nice too. I'm impressed."

A smile twitched at the corner of his mouth. "I'm glad it meets with your approval."

"I better go. I don't want Aunt Carrie to have to wait too long on me. We need to get to the airport in time to get Violet."

He pulled her into his arms. "How about a quick kiss before you leave?"

"I guess I can spare one." His kiss tasted of coffee and cinnamon. After kissing for a long moment, she said, "You already had your morning coffee. I tasted it on your lips."

He looked into her eyes. "I hope someday I'll have my morning coffee with you before I leave for work."

"I better go."

"I'll call you Tuesday evening to see how the road trip's progressing." Samuel walked with her to the front door and waved to Aunt Carrie.

"Bye, Samuel." She gave his hand a squeeze before running to the car.

Aunt Carrie turned the key in the ignition as she buckled her seatbelt. "Samuel did a great job on the picnic table."

"Maybe I'll have him make one for us. We could use another picnic table. Scott and I like to enjoy our backyard with family and friends. I miss not having my own Amish relatives to our house so I'm very glad you're visiting us."

"You were brave leaving everything you knew and taking a chance on an English man." She glanced at her *aenti*. "That didn't come out right. Uncle Scott's always been a nice man."

When the light turned green, Aunt Carrie stepped on the accelerator. "No, you're right. I was taking a big chance. He could've rejected me later, which was always in the back of my mind. I couldn't figure out what he saw in an Amish girl."

"I see why he fell in love with you." Her *aenti* was pretty with a charming and fun personality.

"Oh, we never finished the swimming conversation. I have some bathing suits you might want to wear, or I can take you shopping to buy your own. There are some cute bikinis on sale right now. You have a great figure."

She swallowed hard. A bikini...what was *aenti* thinking? She couldn't parade around in a revealing suit. "I won't be buying a bikini. I was thinking of buying a modest one-piece swimming suit with a billowing skirt."

Aunt Carrie giggled. "I'm sorry. I was teasing you."

She smiled. "That's good. You had me worried for a minute."

"I'm glad you're able to wear a swimming suit. When your mother and I were kids, the girls were only allowed to wear old dresses in the water."

"It's allowed for a sad reason. There were several drowning accidents so the church made swimming lessons available for children. Judith and I took lessons for two summers. Matthew and Noah took them last summer and will again this year."

"I remember Irene telling me how pleased she was about this very progressive approach. It's definitely not found in every Amish community. She said how the bishop realized learning how to swim would prevent many water tragedies."

For a few minutes, both women were lost in their thoughts. Rachel had a feeling Aunt Carrie was remembering her *mamm* too.

After driving on interstate for several minutes, Aunt Carrie broke the silence. "I'm glad you're with me. It's hard on me to visit because it doesn't seem right that my *mamm*, *daed* and *schweschder* are gone. I know it was God's will but I miss them so much. I usually cry a lot on the way back to Lexington."

"Their deaths are one reason I haven't been able to join the church." She bit her lip, thinking how she might as well talk about her *mamm's* death instead of waiting until later. "You laugh more than my mother. And you always have looked younger than she did, even though you are five years older. Do you think her life was too hard and that's why she died from a heart attack?"

Aunt Carrie's eyes never left the highway. After a moment, she changed lanes, then answered, "I couldn't stand being behind that slow car any longer. Going below the speed limit is dangerous too. Irene did work hard, but she enjoyed taking care of her family. She loved you kids."

"It was such a shock because *Mamm* was only forty-four years old."

Her aunt nodded. "I never thought my younger sister would die first. She wrote to me a few days before she died and told me she was tired. I told her to see a doctor. She thought it was because she wasn't sleeping well at night and told me she must be experiencing menopause."

"When I noticed how tired she looked, I helped more so she didn't have quite as much to do in the house." Rachel hesitated asking another question, because she didn't want to offend her *aenti* about English women having easier lives. But she needed to know if Aunt Carrie thought having electricity made a big difference in having a longer life. Did Amish women die younger because of the constant heavy workload? Glancing at her *aenti*, she noticed how smooth Carrie's skin was. With the sun hitting the driver's side of the car, she could see that no gray hairs were interspersed in her aunt's long hairdo. She doubted that Aunt Carrie dyed her hair. Her *mamm's* hair was turning gray before she died. Samuel's mother had a mixture of salt and pepper hair. She seemed to have a worn-out appearance most of the time. Mrs. Weaver had celebrated her forty-fifth birthday last month, but looked more like she was fifty-five years old.

Wearing makeup to cover up a few wrinkles and dark circles under the eyes might shave a couple of years off Mrs. Weaver's face. Amish women never wore makeup. Well, sometimes Katie wore light makeup, but she wasn't a church member yet. Her *mamm* had said to her that it was important not to draw attention to the individual, which can lead to pride. She heard frequently that Amish value the inner beauty which comes from leading a Christian life. It was also practical not to wear makeup, she thought. A woman could spend a lot of money on buying cosmetics.

"I've wondered if losing our parents was too big of a shock for Irene." Aunt Carrie's voice wavered as she continued, "I had a hard time and I wasn't as much part of their lives as my dear sister was. They were such awesome and sweet parents. The buggy accident never should've happened."

"And it didn't even happen at night but during the day."

At the sound of a phone ringing, Aunt Carrie glanced at her before pointing to the cell phone by the drink holder. "Could you answer it for me? It might be Violet."

She nodded when she picked up the Blackberry and saw Violet's face on the screen. She remembered how to use the cell phone because fortunately she'd talked to Violet earlier in the morning. "It's Violet." She pushed the button and said, "Hi, cuz."

"I can't wait to see you, Rachel. We're going to have a blast together at the beach. Tell Mom my flight should be on time. Have you left Fields Corner?"

"We left about forty minutes ago. I'm excited to see you too. How were your finals?"

"I think I did fine. My grades will be posted in a couple of days so I'll be able to check online. I have some plans for us that I hope you like." Violet paused for a moment. "They're calling for the passengers to load now. I have to get on the plane. See you soon."

She closed the cell phone, wondering what kind of plans Violet had in mind for them to do. It didn't matter what they did together, Violet always made everything fun. *Just so none of Violet's ideas will include wild times. I might want to experiment new things, but nothing that will be too earth-shaking. I definitely don't want to smoke a cigarette or drink alcohol.* "Violet said her flight will be on schedule."

"That's good." Aunt Carrie glanced at the clock on the dash. "We should get there before her plane lands. I hope you like our house. I do have electrical appliances but compared to my friends' houses, I keep our home unclut-tered and as simple as possible. But by Amish standards, it will seem a bit overwhelming."

"I'm excited to see where you live. *Mamm* talked about us all going as a family to visit you, but that was one of the things we never got around to doing. Do you think my *mamm* would still be alive if she had left the Plain life?"

"It's hard to know if she'd left her faith, what might have occurred. But I believe it was her time to die. I wish it hadn't been, but I trust God's wisdom. Maybe if she'd gone to the doctor, it might have made a difference but we have no way of knowing that." Aunt Carrie sighed. "I do have it easier when it comes to housework and cooking. I also have a cleaning lady who comes once a month, but I have a lot of mental stress being married to a United States Senator. Each time I give a campaign speech, my heart races. In the beginning I was sure I'd have a heart attack in front of a roomful of people plus the TV cameras and reporters. I hate crowds but yet that's part of my life. Scott has even talked about running for president sometime in the future. That worries me to no end."

"I'm sorry. I wouldn't like having people listen to me while I gave political speeches either."

"I love Scott but if I hadn't met him, I probably would've joined the church and taught Amish children. I wanted to be a teacher, but before that happened Scott came into my life." Aunt Carrie pointed to a McDonald's billboard. "I'm thirsty. I'm going to get a sweet tea at the next exit. I thought we'd stop and eat after we pick up Violet. Is that okay with you?"

"Could we eat at an Applebee's Restaurant? I always hear the English from Cincinnati talk about Applebee's Restaurant when they come to buy our food and furniture."

"Good choice. Violet and I love eating at Applebee's. We can go to one on the way home from the airport." Turning the right turn signal on, Aunt Carrie got off interstate and exited on the ramp.

"I'll pay for our sweet teas."

While waiting in the drive-thru line, Aunt Carrie said, "McDonald's is always busy."

"Did you know that Scott planned on going into politics when you dated him?"

Aunt Carrie shook her head. "He wanted to finish his degree in economics. He got interested in running for a government office after the kids were small. That was another hurdle for me to overcome. Even though, I'd given up my heritage, I couldn't imagine being married to a man involved in government."

"Did you explain that to Uncle Scott?"

"*Ya.* I told him how Amish never run for public office because it violates principles of humility. I explained how Jesus said, 'My kingdom is not of this world.' He tried to understand but he felt an obligation to make the world a better place by being involved in government. The thing is he's great at speaking to citizens. He has this incredible charisma and enjoys solving problems for the average person. He thrives in D.C. and is in his element. But for me, it's another story. I detest it. If I'd known he was going to be a politician, I might not have left Fields Corner. But then I'd have missed out on having Adam and Violet. *Kinner* are such special blessings. We wanted to have a large family, but it never happened. I envied Irene having five children. She loved all of you a lot."

She laughed slightly. "*Mamm* especially loved babies. If a baby was in the room, she rushed to it, like a bee does to honey."

Her *aenti* slightly pushed down on the accelerator, moving her SUV closer to the order screen. Only two cars were ahead of them now. While picking up her purse, she realized Aunt Carrie's resembled hers. Both were simple black purses. She never thought about it before, but even though, her aunt dressed like the English, everything she wore was modest. She looked at her aunt's fingers on the steering wheel. The only jewelry she wore was a plain narrow silver band with a small diamond in the wedding ring plus a simple watch. Was it because Amish women never wore jewelry so her *aenti* felt uncomfortable wearing too much? When Aunt Carrie left Fields Corner, she kept her long curly hair throughout the years instead of getting a short, stylish hairdo. Usually it was worn in a bun like today. Apparently the Bible verse which read that women should have long hair stuck with Aunt Carrie. The only thing missing was a *kapp* covering her head. No bright colors either in her clothes; her aunt looked pretty in a dark green skirt with a beige blouse.

Rachel opened her purse and took money out for their drinks, deep in thought. *It's a surprise to hear how things aren't a bed of roses for my aunt. Had Mamm realized how miserable her oldest sister was about making speeches and all the other things that went along with being in the limelight? Or had Mamm been fooled by the happy image Aunt Carrie projected around them?*

Her *mamm* might have been overworked as a wife and mother, but she had loved her life. Aunt Carrie appeared to have it easier as a married woman in the English world, but was trapped in doing things she had no interest in. And more importantly, she was uncomfortable being the wife of a senator.

Rachel felt sad for her *aenti* because she might have left the Amish community, but her heart was still Amish.

CHAPTER SIX

After glancing at her watch, Carrie said, "Violet should be here soon."

"Aunt Carrie, this airport is awesome."

She smiled at her niece, happy to observe that Rachel's green eyes sparkled with amazement. *I wonder if I looked that thrilled my first trip to an airport terminal.* Rachel's excitement as she stared at the gigantic jets taxi across the runway was like watching a child in a toy store. Some people stared at Rachel's Amish appearance, but that was to be expected. It wasn't every day you saw a Plain person in a busy airport. But Rachel would get looks, regardless of her clothes. *She resembles Irene at that age. A true beauty with fine bone structure and clear skin. It's just as well Scott isn't going to join us in Florida. Scott seems to attract a crowd wherever he goes. Everything must be kept low-keyed and not attract the media's atten-*

tion. David will never allow Judith or the twins to visit me, if anything goes wrong while Rachel's with me.

Family meant everything to her, especially since Irene and her parents had passed on. Having her nieces and nephews visit her was important. Like she'd mentioned to Rachel, she'd been disappointed that God hadn't blessed her with more than two children. She had wanted a large family. Many Amish families had seven children or more, but her parents only had two.

She heard her mother say often that God's ways are not ours and He always knows best.

As Violet rushed toward them, Rachel smoothed her blue dress. "Oh, Aunt Carrie. *Danki,* for picking me up to stay with you. It's already been marvelous spending time with you." Rachel patted her arm. "And now Violet's here with us."

"*Gem gschehre.*" It felt good to say you're welcome in Pennsylvania Dutch. She seldom used any "Dutch" around her family. However, she enjoyed speaking in her Amish tongue when they irritated her.

At the ringing sound of her cell phone, she looked at the caller ID and saw it was Adam. "I better take Adam's call," she said to Rachel and Violet as the girls hugged each other.

Violet rolled her brown eyes at her. "You haven't seen your only daughter for weeks. And already Adam is honing in on my big welcome home moment."

She grinned at Violet. "I noticed who you hugged first, but I'm not complaining. It's nice you two girls are close." She opened her phone. "Hi, Adam."

After Adam answered her questions about his finals, he asked, "Mom, is it okay if I bring Nick with me to the beach?"

"I thought he had plans to go with a group of guys to Florida over spring break." She'd been relieved when Adam had decided to spend time with them at the beach instead. She hated it when he'd gone the previous year to the beach with college kids to party during break. She prayed the whole time he was there, and she'd felt relieved when nothing had happened.

"He wants to spend quiet time with us during break. He's not doing well emotionally and to tell the truth, I'm worried about him."

She hated to say no to Adam's request because Nick's mother had died recently in an automobile accident. It'd been such a shock to Nick and his dad. Glancing at Rachel and Violet busy chatting together, she wondered if David would be upset to know an English man would be at the beach house with his daughter. And Samuel. She hated to think about what he would say to Rachel if an eligible young man was sleeping under the same roof. "Honey, I don't think it's a good idea since Rachel's going to be with us." She heard her son sigh.

"I understand. Samuel called me before Nick asked. He wants me to watch out for Rachel. Samuel said how she's led a sheltered life, but I know it's because he's afraid she'll be like a certain aunt of hers and leave their world."

She chuckled slightly. "Good thing for you and Violet I left, but that doesn't mean I want it to happen to my niece. Let me think about it. I'll call you later tonight. We're at the airport and getting ready to leave."

"Hey, that's another thing. Nick's a pilot and offered to fly me to Florida."

"I didn't know Nick had a plane."

"It's his dad's plane and just a two-seater."

Nick flying her son made her uneasy. "I don't know, Adam. I'd rather you fly on a commercial plane."

Violet touched her shoulder. "Mom, I'm hungry. I haven't eaten since breakfast. Tell Adam you'll call him back when we get to Applebee's."

She gave a nod to Violet while Adam said, "Nick's been flying for years."

In a firm voice, she told Adam, "I'm taking the girls to Applebee's. I'll call you soon." As she led the way to the parking garage, she wondered what to do about Nick. She hated to tell Adam that his friend couldn't stay with them, but it seemed like asking for trouble if she gave her approval. Her niece might be Amish but she was a very beautiful woman. She could see Nick becoming attracted to Rachel. He was a good-looking young man, so it could end being mutual on Rachel's part. In the past, Violet had enjoyed tagging along with Nick and Adam. Nick had always treated Violet as Adam's kid sister. Her daughter was disappointed with the lack of romantic interest from Nick. *How will Violet feel if Nick falls in love with Rachel?*

She pressed the button on her car key to unlock the SUV. *I'm worrying about something that probably won't happen. It especially won't occur if Nick doesn't go to the beach with us.*

* * *

Rachel handed her menu to the young female server, Megan. She liked how Megan had introduced herself to them before taking their orders. If she went back to work at Weaver's Bakery, she should make it a point to introduce herself to the customers. Well, not to the ones in the Amish community. Everyone knew who she was, but the English customers might like to hear her name as she waited on them. Although she did more baking than actual waiting on customers, she might mention it to Katie to introduce herself to the bakery's visitors. She smiled at her relatives. "*Danki.* I can't wait to tell Samuel I ate at Applebee's." She looked at her Aunt Carrie seated across from her and said, "I gave him your phone number, so he can call me. He's calling me tomorrow evening at eight o'clock."

"You can give Samuel my phone number too. I'll tell him if you misbehave when he calls." Violet grinned at Rachel.

"Don't exaggerate anything we do, or we'll have another beach visitor." Samuel might decide to take the bus to Florida if her behavior warrant his intervention, Rachel thought. That would be embarrassing. Her cousin was such a tease.

Aunt Carrie patted her arm. "Samuel understands this is your *rumschpringe.*"

Violet opened her red leather bag and took her phone out of the inside pocket. "I made out a list of things for you to do during your *rumschpringe.*"

"This should be interesting." She leaned closer to read the screen.

"I'll read them so mom can hear my great list," Violet said. "First, on the list is to go shopping for clothes and shoes."

Rachel nodded. "I do want to get a swimming suit. Or I might be able to wear one of Aunt Carrie's one-piece suits."

"That's a relief. I was hoping you wouldn't wear your dress to go swimming in." Violet arched her eyebrows. "Don't take this wrong, but I don't know how you stand wearing those plain black shoes all the time. I want you to get some cute sandals and shoes. Also you have to have jeans and maybe a sundress."

"I don't wear these shoes all the time. We're allowed to wear sneakers." She shrugged. "I don't want to buy too much but would like a pair of capris to wear on the beach and maybe one pair of sandals. I don't need anything else. "

Violet's brown eyes widened. "That's not enough."

"But what will I do with all the new things when I go back home? I guess you could keep them to wear. We seem to be the same size except you're taller."

"Hey, that'll work." Violet gave her a wide smile. "I don't mind if the clothes are shorter on me."

Aunt Carrie said, "Or we can donate the clothes to charity. I think Violet's right about getting several things. And if you decide to wear your Plain clothing most of time, that's fine too."

Violet glanced at her mother before staring at Rachel. "Maybe you'll decide to be English like us...forever."

She'd wondered several times if she could become English; it was hard to imagine leaving her loved ones in Fields Corner. "I want to experience your world, and sometimes I wonder if being English could be better for women. Yet at the same time, I can't imagine not being Amish."

The server brought their spinach and artichoke appetizer with tortilla chips. Violet immediately took a chip and scooped some dip onto it. "I love this." After swallowing a mouthful, Violet glanced down at her cell phone. "Okay, next on the list is makeup. You have such a pretty complexion that I think a little foundation with a light pink lipstick is all you need."

"This spinach dip is delicious." Rachel wiped her lips with a napkin. "I don't know. I've never worn makeup."

"How about just a little lip gloss? That will protect your lips from the hot sun." Aunt Carrie sipped her raspberry tea.

"Or I can just use Chap stick." *Or maybe I should wear makeup. I haven't joined the church yet.*

"Let's move on here." Violet pushed her shoulder length brown locks away from her face. "I didn't put a haircut on the list. I don't want to cause you any problems. I know you aren't allowed to cut your hair."

"*Ya.* I don't think I could do that." Rachel noticed Violet wore several silver rings on her fingers. She had blue dangling earrings with a matching necklace. She glanced at the screen to see if jewelry was the next item. *Whew, no jewelry listed.* Violet must have decided that jewelry accessories weren't necessary with her new English clothing.

"You have to go to a movie." Violet asked, "Or have you already gone to a movie?"

She shook her head. "I haven't. Samuel went to a couple with his friends before he joined the church, but I never have. I'd like to see a movie."

"Rachel, help yourself to more dip." Her aunt continued, "You should get on Violet's or my laptop. I think it'd be nice for you to check out Violet's facebook page too."

Violet nodded. "I have Internet on my list. I want you to see Daddy's political website."

"Something many of my friends did during their running around was they drove cars. Or a few boys drove trucks before they were baptized." Aunt Carrie laughed. "The funny thing is I never wanted to drive and didn't until Scott taught me. We have a long driveway if you want to try driving Violet's car. It's easier to handle than the SUV."

"I'd like that."

"That's all I have, Rachel, but if you think of something you want to try, don't be afraid to ask. I've heard Amish boys try alcohol during their running around, but I didn't add that because I don't drink. I thought you might not want to either." A sad look crossed Violet's lovely face. "My friend, Jenny, died from alcohol poisoning. We were friends ever since kindergarten. She started drinking while she was at college."

"I'm sorry you lost your friend. That's so sad." She put her arm around Violet's shoulders and gave her a hug. She couldn't imagine losing her friend, Katie.

When another woman brought their food, she asked Rachel if she'd ordered the sirloin with garlic herb shrimp. She answered, "Yes, thank you." While eyeing Violet's Mexican chicken, Rachel said, "Your fiesta lime chicken looks good."

Aunt Carrie laughed. "I think Violet gets it each time we eat here."

All three women bowed their heads to pray silently. *It's nice Aunt Carrie and Violet pray silently before meals just like the Amish,* Rachel thought.

They all dug in to eat, and a few minutes later, Violet asked, "Mom, what did Adam want when he called you at the airport? I hope he's still going to Florida."

"He asked if Nick could join us at the beach. Nick's one of Adam's friends," her aunt said to her. "How do you girls feel about that? I'd rather it would just be family, but Nick's having a hard time since his mother died recently."

Violet shrugged. "If we still have a couple of days just for us girls, I don't care. It sounds like Nick needs us."

"Adam's not done with finals for three days, so I'll tell him that we need a couple days after we get to the beach to get groceries and to rest from our long trip." Aunt Carrie's gaze focused on Rachel. "Is it okay with you, Rachel? The beach house is big and they should only be there for a few days."

She couldn't wear her swimming suit in front of Adam's friend. *I'll be too self-conscious showing so much of my body. Well, I'll just enjoy the pool when they aren't there.* "It's okay."

"Should I tell Rachel how hot Nick is?" Violet turned her face away from her mother to look at Rachel. "I used to want Nick to be interested in me. He just thought of me as Adam's little sis. Maybe now that I'm a second year college woman, he'll look at me differently."

"This might not be a good idea." Aunt Carrie jabbed a piece of broccoli with her fork. "Why couldn't their break be a different time? I wonder if they'd like to go to our beach house at Outer Banks instead."

She tucked a loose strand of hair back under her *kapp.* "I'd like to see Adam but that might be nice for us to have a girls' week only at the beach." She'd be disappointed not to see Adam, though. She noticed Violet's amused look. "Or not."

Violet grinned. "Are you afraid you might find Nick more attractive than Samuel? Competition makes life interesting. Samuel might decide to join us at the beach."

"I hope not. I need to experience new things without Samuel. He already mentioned visiting, too, so he could see Adam."

If Nick went to Cocoa Beach, Samuel wouldn't be happy. He needn't worry because she wasn't going to be like Aunt Carrie and fall in love with an English man.

Aunt Carrie never had an Amish boyfriend, or been courted when she met Uncle Scott. *Or had she? Had she broken an Amish man's heart when she married Uncle Scott?*

CHAPTER SEVEN

"All the houses are beautiful but I like yours the best."
Rachel gazed at the Robinson's house as Aunt Carrie
turned into their driveway. The two-story house had
some stone on the front with the rest in brick. She was
impressed with the landscaping and wondered if Uncle
Scott had a green thumb or if Aunt Carrie took care of
the yard work. She imagined that Carrie was in charge of
the outside because of being raised Amish. Gardening
was always the responsibility of women and children
while men and boys did the field work. Obviously, Uncle
Scott didn't have fields to plow, but he wasn't home a lot
to take care of the yard.

"We like it." Aunt Carrie stopped in front of the
garage. "I can see my friend, Marlene, over there working
in her flower beds. I want you to meet her, Rachel. She's
the one loaning us her beach house to use. And I'll just
give her now the baked goods I bought for her."

"Mom, why don't we leave super early in the morning? If we split the driving, we can drive straight through to the beach." Violet leaned forward toward Rachel. "Is it okay we go shopping after we get to Florida for your clothes?"

"I'm in no hurry to get other clothes. I'm anxious to see the beach so I'd love to get there tomorrow." Turning her face away from Violet, she asked her aunt, "I'm sorry I can't help with the driving. I know you'd both go by plane if it wasn't for me."

Violet rolled her brown eyes. "Oh please, how many times have I told you that I love to drive? And Mom doesn't care for flying anyhow. It must be an Amish thing."

"After you two drive thirteen or fourteen hours, I hope you still feel that way. It's stressful when I drive the buggy. I can't imagine driving a car on interstate for hours. Too bad Adam can't go with us and take a turn driving."

"Mom, don't forget to call Adam about Nick tonight."

Aunt Carrie's eyes widened while she stared at Violet. "I certainly hope Nick being around won't be a problem." After opening the car door, she scooted out and yelled, "Hello, Marlene. I want you to meet my niece."

"Geez, Marlene looks pretty excited." Violet grinned while flinging a purse strap over her shoulder. "I guess it's not every day you meet a Plain person."

"She's probably happy you're home and has nothing to do with me." *My cousin's still a tease but that's okay, I love her sense of humor.* After Rachel got out of the car, she saw an attractive woman with short black hair, looking older than her aunt, walk quickly into the yard. Rachel stepped around the car to greet her aunt's neighbor.

While Aunt Carrie introduced her, Marlene removed a garden glove and extended her hand. "I've heard so many wonderful things about you, Rachel. It's a pleasure to finally meet you."

She shook Marlene's hand and said, "It's nice to meet you too. Thank you so much for letting us stay at your beach house."

"I hope you'll have a lovely visit and have fun at the beach." Marlene gave Violet an affectionate look. "I bet you're happy to be finished with finals."

"It's a huge relief. And I can't wait to relax and soak up some sun." Violet hugged Marlene. "How's my second mom?"

"I'm doing great." Marlene kept an arm around Violet as she turned toward her. "Rachel, I happen to have four sons, and Violet's like a daughter I never had." She laughed. "Besides, Violet needs two mothers to keep her in line."

"Violet's blessed to have two terrific women who love her." She liked Marlene and thought how fun it must be to live next door to this delightful lady with four sons. "You've had your hands full. I have three brothers so I know what it's like to live with boys."

Aunt Carrie walked to the back of the SUV. "I got a shoofly pie, cheese, bread and noodles for you. Let's take it to your house."

"Thank you. Everything sounds yummy." Marlene watched Aunt Carrie remove the items of food from the cooler. "That's nice Scott might finish up with his committee work early, so he can join you in Florida."

They were getting their bags out of the car when Aunt Carrie almost dropped the pie. "What? That's news to me."

A flash of surprise crossed Marlene's face. "I thought you knew. Greg called Scott about something this morning, and he told him then. I bet he'll call you this evening. He probably didn't want to interrupt your visit and your drive home."

Aunt Carrie sighed. "Adam's bringing a friend too. So much for our quiet girls' week."

Her *daed* wouldn't like too many English around her during her stay at the beach. But she loved her Uncle Scott and it would be nice to see him again. She had a feeling that her uncle wouldn't be a problem for her *daed*, but Nick at the beach house was another thing. *When Samuel calls tomorrow night, I might leave Nick out of the conversation. If Daed becomes worried, he'll give Samuel permission to take a bus to Florida. That will not help me in my time away from Samuel and family to make my decision whether to join the church.*

* * *

Rachel left the guest bedroom to join Violet in the living room. She looked forward to watching a movie with her cousin. She'd been surprised to learn that her parents had seen this house. They'd stopped once after they went to an Amish wedding in Lexington. She and Peter had been too young to babysit and their grandparents had stayed with them.

"Okay, I have movies I'm planning on taking to the beach, but I thought we'd watch one now. I need to relax after that wild driving lesson." Violet rolled her brown eyes at her.

She laughed at Violet's remark. "Yeah, right. You don't need to relax after my awesome driving. I did so well that I could probably help drive to Florida if I had a license."

"Geez, get an Amish girl behind a steering wheel and she's ready to hit the highway." Violet plopped down on a couch. "Okay, I'm teasing and you did great. I'm glad we drove on a few side streets. It was more fun than driving up and down the driveway. Would you really like to get a driver's license?"

She shook her head before sitting. "Definitely not now. It'd be scary to drive in traffic. And I'd only consider driving if I didn't join the church. I know this will be hard to believe but I enjoy driving a buggy. I like hearing the click-clopping of the horses' hooves as they hit the pavement. It's relaxing."

"But it takes you so long to get anywhere in a buggy."

"It's nice to go a slower pace because you have time to enjoy the scenery. If we need to get somewhere faster, we can arrange a ride with an English driver."

"I thought we'd watch a Reese Witherspoon movie. She's one of my favorite actresses." Violet handed her the DVD. "Hey, you can read the synopsis while I get us something to eat. Would you rather have popcorn or chips to nibble on while we watch the movie?"

"I like both so whatever you prefer is fine."

After reading the movie blurb for "Just Like Heaven," she heard corn popping. Violet must have decided on having popcorn. She glanced around the spacious living room. Cherry hardwood flooring and a few rugs looked nice under the beige and cranberry furniture in the room. She fingered a throw pillow while noticing how the room wasn't cluttered but tastefully decorated. Seeing only a few decorative wall hangings surprised her. Mrs. Maddox's walls were covered with photos and various types of metal hangings. Aunt Carrie did have a few photos on the white fireplace mantel and noticed one showed her grandparents holding Adam and Violet when they were small. She was sure that Grandpa and Grandma Troyer didn't request a picture to be taken with their grandchildren, but they probably didn't see any harm in Aunt Carrie having one of them together. A big family photo of Uncle Scott, Aunt Carrie with their children in a silver frame hung above the mantel.

The electric ceiling fan and the big screen TV definitely wouldn't be in an Amish house. She wondered if her parents had watched TV when they stopped to visit her aunt and uncle. She was glad they'd been here. It was comforting to feel this connection with them. If her aunt had been baptized and a member of the church before marrying Uncle Scott, she would've been shunned. Would her parents have dared to visit Aunt Carrie when that meant going against the bishop?

That was another reason she had waited to join the church; she had to be positive it was the right thing for her to do. She couldn't bear being shunned, but understood why accepting the *Ordnung*, the set of rules and regulations that govern Amish life, were so important. It was serious business to decide to accept the *Ordnung* and become baptized. If afterwards a decision was made to marry someone out of the Amish faith, it would be considered flaunting the church rules. She had heard Bishop Amos recite the passage from Thessalonians when he defended shunning. *"And if any man obey not our word by this epistle, note that man, and have no company with him, that he may be ashamed."*

It was a blessing that Aunt Carrie fell in love with Scott before she accepted the *Ordnung*, but if she hadn't, there would have been other options. In the milder form of shunning, practiced by numerous Amish communities where she lived, the *Bann* was lifted if the individual joined a related Anabaptist-umbrella church, such as a Beachy Amish or more progressive Mennonite church. Many individuals who left their faith did happen to join the Mennonite faith. She bet that Scott and Aunt Carrie might have become Mennonites. Although some Amish disliked the practice of shunning and only performed it symbolically, she didn't want to risk any type of shunning by rushing into joining the church and later regretting her decision.

"Okay, here's our movie food and I brought napkins. I might have gotten a bit carried away with the butter." Violet put the bowl of popcorn on the coffee table.

Aunt Carrie handed her a glass of Coke and said, "I called Adam and they're flying to Florida on Thursday afternoon so we'll have tomorrow night and the whole day on Wednesday without the boys. I want to call that husband of mine next and see what he's got planned."

"Mom, we can wait to start the movie so you can watch it with us."

"No, go ahead. I want to make sandwiches out of the meat and loaf of bread I bought for our lunch. I thought we'd stop and eat at a rest area. That will save some time and break up the trip. I think we'll just hurry eat breakfast at a McDonald's after we drive a couple of hours. We can make pit stops for bathroom breaks and snacks." Aunt Carrie patted her shoulder. "Thank you for baking cookies for us. They'll be delicious to eat on our road trip."

Violet looked at Rachel with admiration in her eyes. "I don't know how you do it. You baked cookies for your dad and I'm sure you did for your brothers too. Plus you baked bread and other stuff ahead to make everything easier on Judith. And knowing you, I bet you cleaned the whole house from top to bottom. I don't think I could ever be an Amish daughter and sister."

"Don't give me so much credit. I love to bake and also I don't want Judith to call begging me to return home. I figured the more I did before leaving would help to keep things running smoothly for a couple of days."

"I'm sure Judith will be fine." Violet said to her mother, "Are we still leaving at five o'clock?"

Aunt Carrie nodded. "We should make good time leaving early, and the weather forecast says no rain and sunny."

"We can go shopping sometime on Wednesday for your clothes." Violet took a handful of popcorn.

"Enjoy your movie," Aunt Carrie said over her shoulder as she left the room.

Violet kicked off her flats. "I was just thinking how if you should decide to become English, you and I'll both be undecided about our future careers. I have no clue what I should do after college. I always wanted to become a doctor, but Adam beat me to it. He's already been accepted at several medical colleges. I'm majoring in chemistry but I need to decide on what kind of a job I want after college."

"You should still go to medical school. Don't let Adam's decision make you give up something you've always wanted to do."

Violet shrugged. "Maybe. But I hate to do the same thing as Adam." She ate a few kernels of corn. "I guess you could still work in a bakery, or have you thought of something you'd love to do if you are no longer Plain?"

While sipping her drink, she thought, what could she do to make a living for herself if she left Fields Corner? "I don't know. I love children so I could follow in your mother's footsteps and take early childhood classes. I think teaching in a preschool might be something I'd enjoy."

"Or you could become an actress like Reese Witherspoon." Violet wiped her fingers on a napkin. "You're beautiful enough, that's for sure. And I never heard of any Amish becoming a movie star so you'd be the only one."

"I'm pretty sure I have no acting ability. When I was in school, I had a small part in the Christmas program and I forgot my lines. I was nervous and kept worrying that I'd pee my panties." She'd been mortified until a prompter finally came to her rescue and whispered a few words to help her to remember the lines.

Violet grinned at her. "We can be beach bums together until we figure it all out."

"That sounds good. It might happen. I can't imagine not loving the beach." *Tomorrow at this time, I'll be looking at the beautiful ocean and white sand.*

Violet stood. "We better get the movie started because we need to get to bed early. I want to take my shower tonight too."

Only attending school through the eighth grade was a problem if you didn't join the church, she thought. *What jobs would be available to me without having a high school diploma? I love to bake so it seems like working in a bakery might be the best choice. But even then, I might have to have more education to work in an English bakery.*

God would direct her to making the right decision about her faith and a career. Her *mamm* had always said that God heard their prayers and He answered them.

Although living on the beach with Violet sounded like fun.

Chapter Eight

Cocoa Beach, Florida

After helping her aunt and cousin carry their bags in from the SUV into the beach house, Rachel said, "I can't wait another second. I'm going to walk and see the beach." She turned away from her relatives to stare out of the patio glass door and was thrilled to see such a gorgeous sun-filled day. She was glad they'd made it to Cocoa Beach before nighttime.

Aunt Carrie nodded. "You do that while I order a pizza. Marlene mentioned to me a few good places to order from. I have their phone numbers in my Blackberry. Are mushrooms and pepperoni okay for the toppings?"

"That sounds good to me." She felt so antsy, wanting to feel the sand beneath her toes.

Violet smiled. "Enjoy the ocean. I'm going to return a few phone calls before going outside."

"See you two in a bit." Rachel slid the glass door open and stepped onto the deck. Staring at the ocean, she was struck with the vastness of it. Taking a deep breath, she enjoyed the smell of the saltwater... so different from home.

As she walked on the beach, a strong feeling of thankfulness came over her. The day was glorious with the perfect weather. The blue water sparkled as the sun's rays hit the waves. The gentle splashing of the waves soothed her spirit. Although the temperature was in the high seventies, the ocean breeze kept her from getting too warm in her dress. In silent prayer, she said, *Dear God, I see the beauty You have created around me. Just as I watch the ocean tides, I know the strong tide of Your love will support me in finding the answers I need before I can commit to marrying Samuel. I want Your will to be done in my life and work always. Thank you for loving me. Through Jesus Christ, Your Lord. Amen.*

She lifted her dress so the bottom wouldn't get wet in the water. While walking in the water, she leaned down to pick up seashells. After having too many to hold in her hand, she decided to take off her *kapp*. Her prayer covering would hold lots of shells. She'd share them with her sister and brothers. And she'd promised to bring seashells back for Katie.

She put her sunglasses back on the top of her head, so she could see everything clearly. She loved feeling the wet sand on her bare feet. Stopping for a moment, she glanced again at the beauty of the ocean. The water stretched as far as she could see to the skyline.

Turning her head toward the house, a thin and dark-haired man caught her eye. She guessed his age to be around late thirties because he looked older than her brother and Samuel but younger than her *daed*. He wore shorts and a T-shirt. He had a camera in his hands which made her realize he'd already taken pictures of her or wanted to. She sighed. *What is with the English and their pictures? It isn't like I'm the only Amish person in the world.*

"Excuse me. I hate to interrupt your obvious enjoyment of the beach, but could I bother you for a minute?"

She could say that he'd already bothered her, and how she was a bit busy at the moment, but picking seashells might not be considered enough of a reason to refuse his request. Besides, she shouldn't be rude. She gave him a small smile. "Sure. I can spare a minute for you."

"I noticed your lovely hat thing and dress. Are you Amish?"

I'll have some fun for once with an English person. It's not like I'll be losing business at Weaver's Bakery by teasing him. Violet mentioned that I should be an actress, so I'll use that excuse for being dressed this way. "I'm trying out Amish clothing for a part in my next movie. I want to feel like an Amish woman so I can do justice to the role I'm going to play."

"I'm impressed. I'm sorry I don't recognize you."

Noticing his raised eyebrows, she wondered if he realized her fib. For one brief second, she considered making up a name that sounded like a movie star. Watching movies with Violet probably had been a bad idea because why else would she lie to this man about being an actress? Her parents raised her to tell the truth. She should be ashamed of herself. Telling a lie was a sin so she said truthfully, "My name's Rachel Hershberger. What's yours?"

"I'm Kevin Sullivan."

She pushed her toes hard into the wet sand. She better fess up about her true identity. "It's nice to meet you. I'm sorry that I lied to you. I'm not an actress. I am Amish."

"Maybe you should consider acting. I believed you and you definitely are pretty enough."

"Hi," Violet said to them.

She turned to look at Violet and felt relief to see her cousin, because continuing the conversation with Kevin Sullivan wasn't something she cared to do. She had a feeling he was buttering her up to ask to take her picture. *Will the English ever tire of snapping pictures of us?*

Violet grinned. "Geez, I leave you alone for a moment and you're already fishing for compliments."

"Violet, this is Kevin Sullivan. And Violet's my cousin." Although it was doubtful Mr. Sullivan would tie Violet to her famous father, Rachel decided to play it safe by not mentioning the last name. And with her uncle arriving on Friday evening, she needed to make sure his name was never mentioned. Aunt Carrie hoped the media wouldn't learn of her husband's weekend visit to Cocoa Beach. Personally, she looked forward to seeing her uncle under happier circumstances. The last two times she'd spent time with him had been during the funerals of her grandparents and her mother.

"Hi. It's nice to meet you," Violet said. "Do you live in one of the private houses here?"

Leave it to her cousin to be blunt to a stranger.

He shook his head. "I'm visiting my aunt, Donna Overton. Your friend Marlene told my aunt that some people would be staying in her cottage. She didn't want my aunt to become concerned with seeing strangers occupying the place. Marlene asked her to keep an eye on the place when they aren't here."

"It looks like you're enjoying taking pictures of this beautiful beach." Violet stared at the water before glancing at his camera. "We've never been here before, but I can see why Marlene and her family enjoy coming here."

A sheepish expression crossed his face. "I did happen to get Rachel in the background of a few." He gave her an apologetic look. "I'm a photographer and I couldn't resist when I saw you collecting seashells. You made the shore scene even more captivating."

Great, he's a photographer. Well, she could understand him taking pictures of the beautiful ocean. She smiled at Mr. Sullivan. "It's okay. The Amish faith does prohibit posing for photographs. If you'd asked for my permission to take my picture, I'd have said no, as this could be construed as a willingness to pose. But I wasn't even aware you took my pictures."

"Thank you for your kindness," Mr. Sullivan replied.

"Hey, it's been nice chatting with you," Violet said to Mr. Sullivan, "but I need to leave soon." She touched Rachel's arm. "I came out here to see if you want to go with me to get the pizza. I decided to pick it up because delivery was going to take too long."

Rachel nodded. "Sure."

* * *

"How was the long road trip?" Samuel asked.

From the balcony, Rachel watched the waves. With the cordless phone held next to her ear, she appreciated Samuel's phone call being right on time. "It was fine." She laughed. "I can't imagine driving a buggy to Florida. You'd definitely have to travel in a car. We made pit stops to use the restroom and to stretch our legs. We did drive for a few hours before we stopped for breakfast at Mc-Donald's. Marlene...*Aenti* Carrie's neighbor, told us a good place to stop at to eat our picnic lunch."

"I bet they loved your cookies." He asked, "Did you go swimming yet?"

"Violet and I swam in the pool. The water felt great." It'd been a long time since she had swimming lessons, so was relieved she hadn't forgotten anything.

"That's good. I guess you got a suit then."

"No, it's a private pool so we went skinny dipping." She couldn't resist teasing Samuel a little.

He didn't respond. *I shouldn't have mentioned being naked in the pool. How embarrassing I said something like that.* "I shouldn't have said that."

Samuel chuckled. "I know you're making that up. If you're not, then you've changed in a matter of hours."

"I'd never go swimming without a suit. I wore *Aenti's* one-piece suit. We haven't gone shopping. We definitely didn't feel like driving too much tonight. Violet's going to take me to the stores tomorrow to buy a few things." She took a deep breath, loving the salty smell of the beach and ocean. "I'm sitting outside right now and loving the view. Cocoa Beach definitely is beautiful. God's made a scenic creation for us."

"That's good. I'm glad you're enjoying yourself. You deserve to get away and to have a relaxing time."

"I might make this a yearly tradition."

"I would like to visit the ocean once a year with you. We could take the bus."

"That might be possible." She paused for a moment, gazing at the seagulls swooping down on the sand. "I needed this time away from my family too. Not just you, Samuel," she said gently. "Even though, it's been a year since my *mamm* died, I didn't have time to grieve. I instantly took over all the things she did. I had to be a mother to Judith, but especially to Noah and Matthew. The boys were so young to lose their mother."

"You've done a great job taking care of everyone. God's good making it possible for you to spend time with your English relatives."

"*Danki* for understanding. I'll pray for God's direction in my life while I'm spending quiet time on the beach." She knew Samuel talked from the business phone that was for his store. His family had a phone in their barn, but Samuel mentioned he decided to work after store hours to call her. She couldn't let go of the fact her *daed* hadn't installed a phone shanty outside their home or in the barn like other Amish families. If he had, her *mamm* might be alive. "Did you get the dining room table finished you were working on?"

"I did which turned into another sale. A husband and wife came into the store today and ordered a dining room table, chairs and a headboard for their new bed. They saw the table I did for the other English couple and were impressed with my work. I'm thankful I can make money from doing something I love."

"Your furniture is amazing."

"If you decide to marry me, I'll get busy making furniture for us."

She sipped from her glass of iced tea. Why did Samuel have to mention their possible future together? She didn't want to talk about making plans for their marriage.

"I'm anxious to start building our house."

She heard the hopeful tone in his voice and wished with her whole heart, she could say what he wanted to hear. She couldn't. She wasn't ready to commit to making wedding plans. "Samuel, I'm sorry I can't give you an answer yet."

"My *daed* said there's no rush. My *mamm* was twenty-one when they married. I need to take his advice. You're worth waiting for, Rachel. I love you."

"Thanks, Samuel. Your patience takes pressure off me. I love you too." She saw Kevin Sullivan walking along the beach. He was occupied with his camera again. He seemed to take a lot of pictures of the ocean. "A man took a picture of me while I was walking on the beach today. Well, not just of me. He was snapping photos of the ocean."

"He probably couldn't resist. You're so beautiful."

She laughed. "I think it was the Amish thing. I was dressed in my Plain clothes, of course. His name's Kevin Sullivan. He's staying in the next cottage with his aunt."

"Is he our age?"

"No, he's older. Maybe in his late thirties."

"Is he married?"

"Hey, don't worry. I'm not into older men." Now that she thought about it Mr. Sullivan never mentioned any wife or children. "I guess he's single. We didn't talk that long."

She heard a loud banging on the other end of the phone.

"I better go. Someone's knocking on the door. I guess they can't see the closed sign."

After saying their sweet good-byes, she thought more about her *daed*. She couldn't let go of his failings as a husband and her resentment of him. Deep in her soul, Rachel knew if she couldn't forgive her father, she would never be able to move on with her life.

* * *

Kevin Sullivan saw Rachel talking on the phone. He'd heard that Amish sometimes used phones. He couldn't believe his luck. When his Aunt Donna mentioned that Senator Scott Robinson's family was staying in the cottage next to hers, he asked if he could visit his favorite aunt. Getting pictures of the popular senator would help his dwindling bank account. Although his aunt wasn't sure if Senator Robinson planned on hitting the beach, he still decided to chance it. But getting pictures of Robinson's photogenic Amish niece was a bonus.

When Rachel neglected giving Violet's last name, he knew she wanted to keep her cousin's identity a secret. Violet seemed a bit mistrustful of him, but being the senator's daughter probably had made her cautious when meeting new people. Maybe he shouldn't have mentioned being a photographer; that might have been a mistake. Violet would mention it to her mother, and they'd be more on guard around him.

He glanced to see if Rachel remained on the deck. She'd left. Tomorrow he'd try to get a few more shots of Rachel and her interesting relatives. He wouldn't be surprised if the charismatic and good-looking senator ran for president in the future. His aunt warned him not to take any unflattering shots of the famous family. She insisted he tell them upfront he was a photographer.

Even though, his aunt said it was only going to be the kids and Carrie Robinson in the cottage, he bet Senator Robinson would join his family. *Why wouldn't he show up at the beach? Senate was out of session. When he arrives, I'll be ready to get some great shots. Then the fun begins.*

CHAPTER NINE

Fields Corner, Ohio

After speaking to Rachel, Samuel opened the door to see who'd been banging on it. He smiled when he saw Rachel's brother, Peter. "Did Ella kick you out of the house? I wouldn't blame her."

Peter rolled his eyes. "Kick me out. Never. That woman couldn't live without me." He stepped inside the store. "I dropped Ella off at the fabric store. She's meeting with the owner about the quilting workshop she's planning on doing there." Peter patted him on the back. "So I thought I'd stop and see you since I'm not a quilter."

"Do you want something to drink? I have bottled water and Pepsi."

"No, *danki.* I can only stay a few minutes. Ella and I don't want to get home late. We don't like to drive at night." Peter arched his eyebrow at him. "I'm surprised you're still working."

"I stayed here to call your sister. I'm going to clean up here and go home soon too. It's been a long day but a *gut* one. Rachel sounded happy that I called."

"How's my traveling sis? Is she in Florida now?"

"*Ya.* She arrived safely. She loves the beach."

"Well, let's hope a different environment helps her to forgive our *daed.* I think that's the main problem. She loves you but she never took the time to mourn completely. It's good she left to have time away from all the demands she puts on herself."

"She's worked hard. No doubt about that. Sometimes I wonder if your mother had lived if we'd be getting married in a few months. But if we don't get married this fall, I hope we will next year." He grabbed a broom and started sweeping wood shavings in the dustpan. He liked to leave the store clean at night.

"*Daed's* going to start building a shanty for the phone. I think one reason he didn't put a phone in before is because they always used Maddox's phone when it was necessary. It's a shame Ella and I hadn't gotten our phone installed earlier. After we married, we couldn't decide whether to put it in the barn or a shanty." He exhaled a deep breath. "But you know, having a phone might not have made any difference. *Mamm* might have died even if an ambulance had gotten there quicker."

He stopped sweeping to look at Peter. "It just tears Rachel apart because it was so unexpected. And your *mamm* was only in her forties."

Peter ran his fingers over the headboard. "I like this. I should have you make one for us. We don't have a headboard."

"Sure, I can do that." The last few days he hadn't been able to shake how Rachel wasn't sure about marrying him. Even though, talking with her made him feel better; it was still a worry with her living in another world. Hopefully, her visit would be for a short time. It was *gut* she hadn't ruled marriage out, but life didn't seem right to him any longer. Rachel wasn't the only unsure person about marriage. Tim seemed to have lost interest in marrying his sister.

"I'll ask Ella but don't know why she wouldn't like this style. It's what most Amish have for headboards." Peter look up from the simple headboard. "How's business anyhow?"

"Quite a few English stopped in today to ask me questions about my furniture and prices. I might have to hire someone to wait on customers if my orders keep increasing. Some days I have to stop working on my furniture to answer questions."

"*Ya.* You should hire some help. You want to get your orders filled in a reasonable amount of time."

After opening the closet door, Samuel put the broom and dustpan away. He turned back to Peter. "You know how in Hebrews, it says that you are supposed to run the race God has set for you and not the race you set for yourself? Maybe it's not God's plan that Rachel become my wife. What if God doesn't think I'm good enough for Rachel?"

Peter removed his hat and ran his fingers through his hair. "You're a good Christian. It's more about timing and God's timetable. I think God brought you two together. Rachel's never been interested in anyone else. She only had eyes for you from the beginning. Don't lose hope and just concentrate on all the good things. You mentioned how Rachel was happy to talk with you, and she just left."

"Thanks. You're a *gut* friend." Although he knew Rachel loved him, he wondered if she could overcome her Aunt Carrie's influence. Then there was also her cousin Violet. Rachel was very close to both English women. "I enjoyed talking with your Aunt Carrie. She stopped in to see me after she bought food from my *mamm's* store. She's an interesting woman."

"She's a thoughtful and kind person. I think Aunt Carrie will be a big help to Rachel seeing how she needs to forgive *Daed* so she can move on with her life. *Aenti* might not be Amish any longer, but she's a parent and knows how important it is to have a loving relationship between children and parents." Peter put his hat back on his head. "I better get back to the store and get Ella. She doesn't want to go home in the dark. Even though, we have flashing lights, she worries an English driver won't see us and hit our buggy."

"You better go and be safe. I'm glad you stopped in to see me."

"Write a letter to Rachel that she'll want to read again and again. When I left Fields Corner to help Grandpa and Grandma Hershberger, I wrote letters to Ella. She told me how much my letters meant to her and how she loved getting them. She said my sensitive letters reinforced her feelings for me and helped in her decision to marry me."

"I told Rachel I'd write to her. I hope I don't have to write too many because she'll be back here soon."

Peter gave him a broad smile. "I love being married to Ella, but cherish this time of being single. You have plenty of time to get married."

After Peter left, Samuel locked up the store. On the way to his buggy, he thought a bit more about his conversation with Rachel. He'd forgotten to tell Peter about the photographer, Kevin Sullivan, taking pictures of Rachel. Sullivan might be innocent in including Rachel with his beach pictures, but there was a possibility he might have an agenda in using them somehow in the media. But Rachel's famous uncle wasn't at the beach with them, so there might be nothing to be concerned about a photographer living next door. Still, he felt a twinge of apprehension about some stranger taking shots of Rachel.

* * *

David peeked into the boys' room and saw they were both asleep. He appreciated Judith reading to them earlier. She continued reading to them from a Hardy Boys mystery that Rachel had started before she left. Judith wanted to finish the book before the bookmobile came again. Fields Corner didn't have a library, so it was difficult for the hard-working Amish families to get to one. It took too much time to drive buggies to check out books.

He was thankful the bookmobile made a weekly stop in Fields Corner. Before closing their door, he took a last glance at Matthew and Noah, remembering how happy they were to have twin sons. *I wish Irene would be here to see them grow up, but for some reason, it wasn't God's plan for my lovely and dear wife to be on this earth any longer. I should be thankful she lived as long as she did and that we had a wunderbaar life together.*

He slowly walked to his own bedroom. Each night he hated to go to bed. He missed his Irene all the time, but night was the hardest on him. Irene had snuggled next to him. While they held each other in their arms each night, they'd talked about how their day had gone. A few nights before she died, their conversation had been about Judith. Peter had just married Ella and Rachel was seeing Samuel, so Irene was happy about their two oldest children. She was hopeful that a marriage would occur between Rachel and Samuel. Her worry had been about Judith. Although she was proud of Judith's decision to be a teacher, she'd been dismayed at their daughter's wish for more education. Apparently Judith had seen English young women carrying college books. She'd told Irene that she would like to continue her education.

He wondered what Irene would think now that Rachel was the daughter unsure about joining the church and getting married, because of him being a poor *ehemann*. From Proverbs 22:6, it said, "Train up a child in the way he should go: and when he is old, he will not depart from it." He hoped this verse would prove true in Rachel's case, and she wouldn't be like the few adult children who left their Amish upbringing to live in the English world. Judith hadn't mentioned again getting her GED and going away to college. She decided teaching in the Amish school was the only place she wanted to be, and he'd been relieved when she'd talked to Bishop Amos about joining the church. Fortunately, Peter hadn't given them any problems before he was baptized. He'd never gotten drunk like some of the boys his age during *rumschpringe.* His English friend, Fred Maddox, said that all teenagers rebel sometimes, but his Peter had done little to worry him and Irene.

Before removing his suspenders, he glanced at the bed again. He couldn't imagine sharing it with another wife. That morning, his friend, Amos had visited to talk to him about getting married again. His sister Barbara had lost her husband, and Amos told him, "You still have young children. You should think about getting a wife to help raise Matthew and Noah."

"I'm sorry your sister lost her spouse. Rachel has done a fine job with helping me with the boys. Also Judith's close to them and gives them extra attention too. We're doing as well as can be expected after losing Irene."

Amos said, "Apparently, Rachel has felt the pressure of taking care of them since she's not here. Judith will take on more teaching responsibilities after she joins the church. Rachel might have her own home soon. She won't be able to take care of the house and the boys as much if she marries. My sister's going to visit soon. You remember her...she used to follow us around. Barbara doesn't have children but she'd make a fine mother to yours. It's been a year now, David. Everyone's out of mourning. It's time to think about your family's future."

"I'll think about what you said. *Danki*, for stopping by to see me." He noticed his friend's thinning white hair. They were the same age but Amos looked older. Amos made a good leader for their district, but right now he wished Amos wasn't his bishop.

He didn't want to court Barbara. He didn't want a new mother for his boys. They'd already had the best *mamm* in the world, and she couldn't be replaced by someone else.

I'd feel like I'm betraying Irene if I courted and married someone else. She'll always be in my heart.

Listening to Bishop Amos was a bit hard because of their past. They'd been childhood friends and gotten into trouble together. Nothing terrible but enough scrapes to give their parents a few gray hairs. As young adults, Amos came to him whenever he had any questions or needed help with any problem. Amos had even followed him to Fields Corner when he left their childhood community. He felt uneasy sometimes with the reversal of roles. But he had remind himself that Amos's selection was based on "divine appointment" through the drawing of lots, as shown in Acts.

It was difficult seeing the stern look in his old friend's eyes. Amos, of all people, should realize he wasn't ready to marry again. Especially Barbara. She'd gotten under his skin a few times while they were growing up. She'd been like an itch that could never be scratched enough. Even Amos had said how they needed to pray for her husband when she married, and they had moved to Indiana.

Although it'd been a long work day, he didn't feel like going to bed. *I'll go talk with Judith. She's in the kitchen grading papers.* He had a special bond with his youngest daughter. When she'd been eight years old, Judith came down with double pneumonia. Because Irene was busy taking care of their baby boys, he'd spent the most time at the hospital with Judith.

As he walked down the stairs, he grinned when he thought of a way he could escape seeing Amos's sister. He could take the boys and Judith to visit Carrie in Kentucky. Going to see his parents wouldn't work because they'd suggested a month ago he should remarry. But Carrie wouldn't bother him with marriage suggestions. She was a good listener.

When he entered the kitchen, he noticed the dark circles under Judith's eyes. "Daughter, you should go to bed. It's getting late. You won't have any energy to teach if you stay up any later."

Judith glanced up at him and smiled. "I could say the same thing to you. You should be in bed. You milk the cows at four-thirty."

"I wanted to go to bed but knew it was pointless to try and sleep yet."

"We should talk then." She pointed to the chair across from hers. "Sit for a moment while I put my papers away. What's keeping you up? It can't be my cooking yet. I fixed Rachel's casserole the first night, and Ella brought over the stew for this evening's meal."

He lowered himself into a chair, and exhaled a deep breath. "Too many thoughts keep me from sleeping some nights. This is one of those nights. During the day, I keep busy with work, but at night I can't stop thinking about your *mamm*. I miss her so much."

Judith squeezed his hand. "I'm sorry."

"Bishop Amos didn't help my frame of mind today. While you were at school, he stopped by." He told Judith what the bishop said about remarrying, but how he couldn't imagine being married to another woman.

"I'm surprised because he should know that Rachel and I are here to help with Matthew and Noah." She gave him a thoughtful glance. "He must think you and his sister might enjoy each other's company. I don't see how she could do a better job than we are with the boys. She hasn't had any experience with raising children. But I don't blame you for not being interested. You and *mamm* were together for a long time and were great together."

"I wasn't a *wunderbaar ehemann*."

"*Daed*, don't think that way."

"Rachel left here because she faults me for your *mamm's* death." Never had he felt that Judith blamed him, but he needed to hear what his younger daughter thought.

"She also left because she's always wanted to see the ocean. Away from us should help her to think things through. I'm hoping staying with Aunt Carrie and Violet will take her bitterness away." Judith slid her students' papers into a folder. After a pause, she continued, "For a short time, I was angry at *Mamm*. I overheard Mrs. Maddox offering to drive her to an English doctor for a checkup. *Mamm* refused and said she'd go later. She had an opportunity to go and she didn't take it."

"That's because she wanted me to take her to the doctor. She knew Mrs. Maddox had her hands full with the new baby."

She frowned. "I know except if it'd been one of us ill, *Mamm* wouldn't have hesitated to impose on Mrs. Maddox to drive us to the doctor." She sighed. "But I decided it was wrong of me to be angry at *Mamm*. I decided to be grateful for the time we did have together."

"I'm building the phone shanty this week. I should've done it long time ago."

"That will be helpful if I need to make calls for school stuff."

He nodded. "I wanted to put one in a few years ago, but your *mamm* didn't want one. She said it was an extra expense that we didn't need. I think she enjoyed going to the neighbors to use their phone when she made doctor appointments for you *kinner*. She had a close friendship with Mrs. Maddox."

Judith's raised her eyebrows in disbelief. "I didn't know she was the one not wanting a phone. We assumed it was you. But now that I think about it, she did like visiting Mrs. Maddox, even more with the new baby."

"I should've insisted about the phone, but when it came to household matters, I yielded to your *mamm's* wishes." He gave Judith a small smile. "We were a team and made decisions together about family matters and any important business decisions."

Leaning closer to him, she said, "Rachel doesn't realize *Mamm's* the reason we never had a phone."

He shrugged. "The phone's not the only reason she's angry at me. Even if I tell Rachel your mother didn't want one, she'll still say I wasn't a good husband."

"I think Rachel will come to her senses when she's on the quiet beach. God will speak to her, and she'll see that being angry at you is wrong." She patted his hand. "This time away will give her a new perspective about everything."

"That's what Peter said too. I hope you're both right." He didn't want to lose Rachel. He loved his eldest daughter, even though she didn't seem to love him right now.

CHAPTER TEN

Rachel carried an insulated cup of coffee outside with her. She couldn't wait to walk on the beach so she could enjoy the morning sun before cooking breakfast for her *aenti* and cousin. She wanted to surprise them before they left to go shopping. She hadn't been able to help with the driving, but cooking them a *wunderbaar* breakfast was something she could do. Marlene's neighbor had put a dozen eggs and bacon in the refrigerator. She'd use their Amish cheese to make omelets. She was glad they also brought a loaf of bread with them so she could serve that, too, with her big morning meal.

She was dressed in tan capris and a green top of Violet's. She felt strange not wearing a dress. The capris weren't feminine enough for her. In the Bible it said that women should not dress as men. She and other Amish women never wore pants because of this reason. She glanced down at Violet's capris. These were also a bit fancy with a button adornment on the cuff of each leg. Buttons were never used on Amish dresses. But Violet told her it was time to go English, because it'd be easier to try on clothes without wearing her Plain clothing. Violet had watched her yesterday while she removed her dress using straight pins. Her cousin couldn't believe that Amish women didn't put zippers or buttons on their dresses.

"Why?" her cousin asked while she'd watch her remove the straight pins from her dress.

"Because buttons are forbidden on certain items because of a couple of reasons," she'd answered. "One Amish objection is because of the association with military uniforms. During the Middle Ages, the buttons on soldiers' shirts were switched from the left side to the right side. This change allowed the soldier to unbutton his coat more quickly to draw a sword. As you know, Amish are devout pacifists. By the way, mustaches have a long history of being associated with the military, so that's why you never seen an Amish man with a mustache."

"What's the other reason for no buttons?"

"The ban on buttons goes back to the days in Paris when they were a fashion rage and a way to display wealth. The buttons were costly and showy, so the church leaders made a ban on buttons. But we can use hook-and-eye closures. Since I'm adept at using pins, I skip sewing the hooks and eyes in."

"If buttons are a symbol for vanity in your faith, then why does Uncle David and your brothers have buttons on their shirts?"

"That's true about men's shirts fastening with traditional buttons. It's just always been this way. Their suit coats and vests fasten with hooks and eyes. Their pants are made with a flap in the front held closed by buttons to avoid the use of a zipper. Zippers are just not allowed."

As her feet hit the sand, she heard someone ask, "May I join you?"

She turned and saw Kevin Sullivan. *He's already up at six o'clock in the morning. Oh great, is he always going to be around when I'm outside?* He seemed nice enough but she didn't feel like talking. She'd wanted to enjoy God's beautiful sky and feel the warmth of the sun's rays while praying for her family...and for herself. She needed to be surrounded by quiet and concentrate on hearing God's answers to her prayers. More than anything, she wanted to understand why she couldn't move on with her life. It'd been a year since her mother passed on. *Mamm shouldn't have died from a heart attack, but by now I should've come to terms about it.* But it wasn't just her mother's death that saddened her, she missed her grandparents too. She'd spent time with them on a regular basis. They were the sweetest couple.

She gave a quick nod, noticing he didn't have his camera. *At least he won't be snapping my picture this morning.*

"It's peaceful this time of the day."

It was until you joined me. "Yes, it is."

"Hey, look at this big shell." After Mr. Sullivan picked up the shell, he handed it to her.

She examined it, liking the pink color. "It's pretty."

"Keep it for your collection."

"Thanks. Have you gone to a lot of beaches?"

"I've been to a few. Last summer I went to Outer Banks for the first time and I really liked it there."

"I'll have to remember that. Maybe I'll get to Outer Banks someday."

For a few minutes neither said a word while they both continue walking. Then Mr. Sullivan broke the silence.

"I noticed you aren't wearing your Plain clothing." He grinned at her. "Are you allowed to wear English clothing when in Florida?"

"So you aren't just interested in taking pictures... you like to ask questions about my faith."

"I like to learn about different lifestyles. You have to admit the Amish are appealing to the general public because of the way you dress. And the fact you don't use electricity."

"I think the English are much more interesting. They spend hours telling everything they are doing during the day on Facebook. Violet showed me her Facebook page and how her friends tell so many details about their daily lives. And I watched Violet tweet constantly on our way here." She cleared her throat. "It seems to me that precious time is wasted each day by having electricity and the Internet."

He chuckled. "I don't spend much time on Facebook, but you do have a point. My sister takes time to post on

Facebook on how she's going to take a nap. I'm not sure why that's important for people to know."

I should explain why it seems we're doing without, but in fact, we are gaining a closeness to God by not using electricity. "We get along without all the modern conveniences because it keeps us focused on God. While doing our daily tasks slowly, we have time to pray and concentrate on God's goodness to us. We value simplicity because it gives us a chance to live a slower-paced lifestyle. In order to keep separate from the world and maintain our self-sufficiency, we avoid owning cars and using electricity." She smiled. "We don't have to worry about power shortages when it storms."

"A lot of Amish have their own businesses, so they must use electricity in their stores."

"We use gas instead of electricity. Gas-powered refrigerators and stoves are used in our homes and businesses. Our equipment for milking our cows runs on propane and not electricity." She remembered how happy her *daed* and *bruder*, Peter, were when Bishop Amos gave them permission to upgrade their milking operations, so they could have Grade A certification for their dairy farmers' milk.

"That's good you don't have to use wood stoves to cook your meals." He raised his eyebrows. "I've seen Amish riding in cars, so it seems hypocritical to say it's wrong to own them."

She nodded. "That's because Amish realize sometimes it's necessary to travel further than a buggy allows. It would've taken too long to come here by buggy. We sometimes hire drivers for transportation to the hospital, for large shopping trips and to visit relatives living far away. But we believe that when a family owns motor vehicles, mobility is made much easier and that isn't a good thing for us. Family members may spend extended periods away from home, and this has a huge negative effect on families."

"I read once that Henry Ford said something similar after he saw how his invention had caused adverse changes in families by causing them to go different directions instead of spending time together."

A lot of non-Amish people thought they were opposed to technology itself, which wasn't the case. *I should explain in more detail about our beliefs to Mr. Sullivan since he seems interested in learning about my faith.* "We don't shun technology because we find it evil within itself. We oppose it because rifts might be created within our community if we use certain types of machinery. For example, the Amish don't use tractors because it might encourage farmers to buy more land, when they see they can plow faster and get more crops planted. That would cause tensions within our communities."

* * *

Carrie smelled the coffee as she walked into the kitchen. Rachel must've made coffee, knowing she'd never sleep late. She'd mentioned to Rachel how she never could sleep later than six-thirty in the morning. Marlene had a collection of colorful mugs on a rack. When she went to get a cup, she saw a handwritten note on the counter and read: *I'm going to take a short walk on the beach. I'll be back to fix breakfast. Rachel*

She thought about joining her niece on the beach. She'd always thought that walking during the early morning hours was a grand way to start your day. But one problem, she'd better change into something else. Even though it was early, she didn't want to take a chance on someone seeing her in pajamas. Before changing, she walked outside on the balcony to see if Rachel had just left. Her eyes widened at the sight of Rachel walking with a thin and dark-haired man. She squinted her eyes to see if she could see more of him. He wasn't carrying a camera so she wasn't sure if he could be the photographer. Violet had briefly mentioned to her about someone named Sullivan taking pictures of Rachel, but it'd been after Marlene had called to see if they'd arrived safely.

"Good morning, Mom."

She turned to smile at Violet. Her daughter looked as if she just crawled out of bed and wore lavender pajamas. "What are you doing up so early this morning?"

Violet sighed. "I can't sleep in like I used to. Remember, how I could sleep until early afternoon on the weekends while in high school. Does that mean I'm an adult now?"

She laughed. "I never heard of that being one of the criteria in being considered an adult, but maybe it is."

"I wonder who's with Rachel." Violet leaned closer to the railing. "Great. That photographer's hanging around her again. I bet he knows Dad's a senator. Do you think he's trying to get information from Rachel about us?"

She frowned. "I hope not. Marlene promised me that we could spend a quiet time here with no press hounding us. I better give her a call this morning and ask her if she knows anything about this Sullivan guy."

"I bet the neighbor never mentioned to Marlene that her photographer nephew was going to visit her."

While Violet watched Rachel walk with Sullivan, she asked, "Do you feel differently about your choice now that Rachel's spending time with us? I'm sure it's a reminder of what you lost when you got married. I know it had to be hard for you to leave your family and faith to marry Dad."

"I'd make the same decision all over again, but there have been times when I miss some things about the Plain life." She squeezed Violet's shoulder. "I'm thankful God blessed us with you and your brother. I have a wonderful family and a great life. Nothing is ever perfect, and I've learned to accept your dad's desire to serve our country as a Senator."

Violet grinned. "Just think if Dad would've converted and became Amish, we'd be living a whole different life. Can you picture me without my electronic devices?"

"I can picture that easier than seeing your father in Plain clothing. He likes his designer suits and ties, but he definitely enjoys golfing in casual pants and shirts. And I can't imagine him doing any Amish type careers. But he has a strong faith in God like my father did. Those two enjoyed talking about the Bible and prayer. Your father has always respected my Amish upbringing."

Violet's brown eyes filled with concern. "One thing about being an Amish woman is you don't have to go to college. I don't know what I'll ever do with a degree in chemistry. I don't want to teach and there's nothing I'm excited about doing with science after I graduate."

"You still have time to figure it all out. Maybe you can shadow a few careers that require a science background and see if that helps you to make a decision." She patted Violet's arm. "We need to pray for God's guidance."

"Good, it looks like Rachel's ditching Kevin, the camera man. She's heading back. I'm hungry. I saw her note about cooking breakfast." Violet played with her drawstring on her pajamas bottoms for a moment. "It's actually weird to see her wearing my capris. My whole life I've seen my cousin in dresses and aprons." Violet glanced at her. "Mom, I know Amish never take pictures, but I've always wished I could see pictures of you as a little girl."

She gave a quick nod. "Amish believe that photographs in which they can be recognized violate the Biblical commandment, 'Thou shalt not make unto thee any graven image.' I'm glad I took a couple of pictures of Irene on her last visit to our house."

"Have you shown Rachel the pictures?"

"Not yet. I'll give her a picture to have and she can keep it hidden somewhere. She should have a picture of her mother. I'll give it to her soon."

"Do you think Rachel will stay much longer with you after my spring break is over?" Violet asked.

"It's hard to say. I know she needs time to work through her feelings about a lot of things. She might stay with me at home for a short time before going back to Fields Corner."

They became quiet while watching Rachel walk slowly through the sand.

"Good Morning, *Aenti* and Violet." Rachel gave a broad smile to them, as she reached the top step. "I timed it just right. Hope you two are hungry."

It was lovely to see her niece smile and look happy. She was thankful to have Rachel here on the beach with them, but felt nervous about Sullivan talking with her again. After breakfast and after the girls left to go shopping, she needed to call Marlene to see if she knew anything about the photographer.

"We saw your note but you don't need to cook. This is your vacation." Carrie knew Rachel had worked hard trying to take Irene's place in the Hershberger household. Rachel needed to relax and enjoy her free time.

"You and Violet had to do all the driving here." Rachel grinned at Violet. "And I want you to have enough energy to drive me to the stores. While we shop remind me to buy postcards."

"What about Samuel? Does he get a postcard from you?" Violet asked.

Rachel blushed. "*Ya.* He definitely gets one from me."

Violet tucked her hair behind her ears. "Hey, you and Mom should teach me some Pennsylvania Dutch phrases and words, so we can use it in front of the guys. It'll drive them crazy not knowing what we're talking about."

Rachel slid open the door to enter the kitchen. Over her shoulder she said, "Sure. We can use it in front of Mr. Sullivan, too, but probably won't work. He's so interested in anything Amish that he'll want to know what each word means."

Carrie followed Rachel into the kitchen. "What kind of questions did he ask about being Amish?"

"Just the usual stuff. Why we ride in cars but won't own them and about not using electricity." Rachel opened the refrigerator and removed a package of bacon. "It was nice of your friend to tell Mr. Sullivan's aunt to stock the refrigerator with eggs and bacon. I thought I'd make omelets for you both."

"*Danki*." She glanced at her daughter. "That's Pennsylvania Dutch for thank you."

"Omelets will be *wunderbaar*," Violet said, looking pleased with herself. "I wonder if Pennsylvania Dutch's offered at my college. That would be cool to get credit for learning it."

While refilling her coffee, Carrie glanced out the window and saw Mr. Sullivan still on the beach. *Why was he staring at their cottage?* "I wonder why Mr. Sullivan is watching our place," she said to both girls.

Rachel put a stainless steel skillet on the burner. "I did hate seeing him on the beach this morning. I wanted to pray and enjoy God's handiwork while walking along the beach. But Mr. Sullivan asked if he could walk with me. I forgot to tell you that he mentioned me not wearing my own clothing."

He might be harmless in asking her niece questions about her faith, but something occurred to her. What if he sold pictures of Rachel with her in Plain clothing, and also in Violet's clothes? David would not be happy. Of course, Rachel wasn't wearing something like a bikini, so shouldn't be a big deal with her not being baptized yet. *But will David even see the photos if this should happen?* He only read *The Budget*, the Amish paper. While many newspapers were failing, *The Budget*, continued to thrive. It was a weekly paper published on Wednesday, and she subscribed to it. She enjoyed the articles written not by paid journalists but by hundreds of Amish volunteers called "scribes." Judith had written a few stories for *The Budget*.

Or what if Sullivan was using Rachel to fabricate lies about them? She turned away from the window. "Rachel, did Mr. Sullivan take any pictures of you today?"

Rachel stopped cutting up a tomato. "No. He didn't have his camera this morning."

Why couldn't photographers and news people leave them alone? But of course, she knew why. She was married to a popular politician. She sipped her coffee, thinking how she wanted this week on the beach to be a fantastic vacation for Rachel. A carefree time. Her niece deserved to have a relaxing time. She was feeling regret coming to Cocoa Beach. *Maybe we should've gone to Myr-*

tle Beach instead and stayed at our own place. It wouldn't have been as warm but with the heated pool, the girls would've enjoyed swimming and still could have enjoyed walking on the beach.

* * *

Kevin Sullivan, shoving his hands in his pockets, turned to walk back to his aunt's house. Feeling a little guilty about what he planned to submit to the media about the Robinsons surprised him. Invading their privacy was his job. He couldn't afford to have a change in his plans. He spent money flying here when his aunt told him how Carrie Robinson would be living next door for a week. He wasn't made of money, like some people. His life had never been easy, that's for sure, with his father bailing on their family. Sometimes he wondered where the jerk was now. But Robinson came from a wealthy family with great parents from what he'd learned while researching them. Interesting that he chose a woman with such a different background. Did Robinson have it in the back of his mind that a woman like Carrie Robinson would be appealing to the voting people? Although Robinson wasn't a politician when he'd married her, that thought could've been in the back of his mind. His political ambition might have been a goal in selecting his future wife.

He had it from a good source that the Senator and his son would be arriving soon but in the meantime, getting pictures of Violet Robinson and her cousin might prove to be fruitful.

But he needed pictures of Carrie Robinson too. She hadn't been outside except on the balcony knitting something yesterday. Boring. He wanted a shot of her in a swimming suit. She'd been photographed a lot in her simple but elegant clothes. No one had ever gotten a shot of her in anything less than formal clothing. He'd told Rachel how he was driving his Aunt Donna to the store, so hopefully she mentioned that to her aunt. He'd like her to feel safe and venture outside while she thought he was away.

Senator Robinson was a lucky man. Carrie Robinson was a beautiful woman with an interesting childhood. In doing his research last evening, he'd learned that Amish had a choice whether to join their church, or to live in the outside world. He found it interesting that Amish babies are not baptized at birth, but make their own choice when older whether they want to join the church and become baptized. Although it was helpful to research the Amish online, he was glad to get information directly from an Amish person. He'd have more credibility for his article with a real live Amish person sharing what it was like being in her world.

If Rachel met a young man, it'd be even better. Anything Amish seemed to make the news these days. People had diverse opinions about them and were enthralled with them driving buggies for their transportation.

Tapping into the Amish perspective until the even hotter news was available should pay off in huge dividends for him. He desperately needed the money. When the Senator arrived he'd be ready with his camera. Even though he could tell Violet was mistrustful of him, it was a free world and they couldn't stop him from taking pictures.

Chapter Eleven

Rachel loved her new one piece swimming suit. Or swim dress as Violet called it. She almost didn't buy it, though, when Violet said in the fitting room that the Calvin Klein style was flirty while still covering her hips and breasts. *I don't want Adam's friend, Nick, to think I'm flirting with him, but hopefully he'll never see me in this suit.* She wasn't sure about wearing her new capris and tops around the guys either. Maybe switching back to her clothing would be for the best. Feeling free from her Amish upbringing and being on the beach didn't mean she had to give up her Plain clothing. She understood why Violet wanted her to experience as much as possible during her *rumschpringe*, but she might feel a bit more comfortable without too many changes.

"Rachel, you should reapply some sunblock." Her *aenti* pointed a knitting needle to the bottle of sunblock on a small table by the pool. "The Florida sun is stronger than what we're used to. I don't want your fair skin to get sunburned."

Violet looked up from her magazine. "Yeah, it won't take you long to put more lotion on your face and what little skin shows."

"Hey, a lot of me is exposed." She stopped swimming and rested her hand on the side of the pool. "Remember, Violet, I'm usually in a dress to my ankles."

"I love your suit. It has long classic lines and isn't frumpy at all." Aunt Carrie stopped knitting to glance at Violet in her bright red bikini, stretched out on a lounging chair. Aunt Carrie, wearing a one-piece black suit, said, "I'm relieved you didn't get a suit like my daughter's."

"Well, maybe if Nick sees me in this bikini, he'll realize I'm not just Adam's little sis." Violet sighed, a long dramatic one. "I can't wait to see Nick."

Aunt Carrie gave Violet a thoughtful look. "Honey, don't get your hopes up. He's probably not going to be himself. He's having a hard time dealing with his mother's sudden death."

"I wasn't thrilled when I first learned Nick was coming, because I wanted a quiet time with you two and Adam, but I realize that was selfish of me." Using the ladder, Rachel climbed out of the pool. "It's great that Adam thought to include Nick."

"I think it'll be a blessing for you and Nick to share some of your feelings about your mothers with each other... but only if you're both comfortable with this." Aunt Carrie took a sip of iced tea. "If he needs to vent to me, I'll be ready too. Even though, my parents were older when they died, it was still unexpected and difficult. I miss them so much at times."

"I can't imagine losing you or Dad," Violet said. "It's heartbreaking that Grandma and Grandpa Troyer and Aunt Irene aren't with us any longer."

"Did I ever tell you that my sweet *mamm* finished a wedding quilt for me? It's beautiful and before her death, she told me how much she enjoyed making it for me and Samuel. I'll always cherish it even if I don't marry Samuel."

"That's what worries me. You aren't engaged to Samuel." Violet's voice wasn't her usual upbeat tone but serious. "Just don't fall for Nick."

Grabbing a beach towel, she frowned at Violet. Her cousin should realize there was not any possibility of her falling in love with Nick. For one thing, she wasn't about to date an English young man. She needed to concentrate on making a decision whether to marry Samuel in the upcoming fall or winter months. What a relief that Nick and Adam wouldn't even be around that long. She hated seeing Violet concerned that she'd go after Nick. Why would she even think that? She'd never want to hurt her cousin.

"I'm not going to be interested in Nick. I do love Samuel. I'm just not sure my love is strong enough to get married to him right now. I have a lot to work out first in my own life before making any commitment." She squeezed Violet's arm. "Besides, you're like my *schweschder.*" Rachel paused to see Violet's reaction to her word for sister.

"*Schweschder* means sister," Aunt Carrie explained.

Rachel continued, "I'd never flirt or do anything to make Nick think I'm interested in him becoming a boyfriend."

Violet shrugged. "Sorry but I don't think you realize how gorgeous you are...you might not fall for Nick but I can see him wanting to spend time with you. Plus you're so mature for your advanced age." She grinned a little. "You're only a little older than I am, but sometimes I have it over you, cousin... or *schweschder.*"

She laughed. "How's that?"

"Yes, I'm interested in this explanation." Aunt Carrie stopped knitting and glanced at Violet.

Violet closed her magazine. "It's true you've been taking care of your siblings while I've been attending college." Violet sat up straighter in her chair after she glanced at both of them. "I've taken care of several immature freshmen since starting college. Many freshmen go crazy after being cut loose from family and being on their own. I don't party like they do. My roommate's gotten ill several times from partying and drinking too much. She also has loose morals and picks up random guys and brings them to our room. I've tutored students struggling in their science and math courses. I've done all this while adjusting to living away from home... and trying to keep my grades high. It hasn't been easy."

Aunt Carrie gave Violet a worried look and said in a firm voice, "You should've told us about your roommate.

You shouldn't have to put up with that. You needed to move out of that room months ago. Or Laurie should've been the one to get out. I can't believe you never said a word about any of this."

Violet shrugged. "I didn't want to worry you and Dad. I'm not going to room with Laura again. When we had to get our room requests in for next school year, I requested my friend, Tanya, to be my roommate. I met her in my science class." Violet grinned before she said, "She's a nerd, like me."

"I can't imagine leaving home and being in a dorm. I've always been surrounded by family. This is my big escape from Fields Corner but I'm still with family." Would she be able to cope as well as Violet in a similar situation? she wondered.

Aunt Carrie patted Violet's arm. "I'm proud of you that you didn't give it to peer pressure."

"Even though it seems our worlds are completely different, some Amish teenagers do go a bit wild during their *rumschpringe*. Maybe not as serious as some of the stuff that your college students do. All I know is that some do cut loose and drink alcohol. Their drinking might get them into serious trouble with the law. Then this type of behavior gets portrayed in the news. But *rumschpringe* shouldn't be depicted this way as being a time of wild partying. It's the exception rather than what normally occurs. At least, in our district it doesn't happen often."

"Did Peter and Samuel try alcohol?" Aunt Carrie asked.

She shook her head. "I don't think so. Both did drive cars a few times, go to baseball games and movies but otherwise, they weren't interested in anything not Amish. And many don't experiment in your world at all, but attend Sunday sings after church and play volleyball games." She smiled. "I have a mean serve."

"Hey, we can challenge Adam and Nick to a volleyball game." After Violet gave her a pleased glance, she turned to her mom, "You and Dad can play too."

"Sounds like fun. Dad and I can use the exercise."

"Do the teenagers actually sing at these Sunday evening things?" Violet asked.

Rachel nodded. "Yes, they do but it's more than just singing. Usually there are outdoor activities included for the young people. In the fall, there are bonfires and hayrides. In the winter we enjoy sledding and ice skating while in the spring and summer, we take long walks and have picnics. Amish teens get restless and we feel the same things any other teens do. Spending time at the singings with other young people helps us to find the right person to marry."

"So is that the main purpose of the Sunday get-togethers to find your future spouse?"

"The weekly events are special because Amish youths from surrounding districts come together to socialize. This gives a boy a chance to arrange a date with a girl. Usually the first date will be him taking her from the singing that evening. Of course, that's after he's asked the girl if he can drive her home in his buggy." She paused for a moment. "But to answer your question, the get-togethers are to provide a time to find someone whose personality and character will mesh with your own in hopes of creating a Christian home which God will bless."

"That's sweet." Violet arched her eyebrows. "Is that how you and Samuel started dating?"

"*Ya*. I was so *froh* when he escorted me home after a singing in his courting buggy."

"What's a courting buggy?"

At the ringing of her cell phone, Aunt Carrie put down her knitting project to glance at her caller ID. "I better get this. It's Marlene returning my call. I've been hoping she'd call me to tell me what she's learned about our nosy neighbor."

After Aunt Carrie left to go inside to talk, Rachel answered, "The courting buggy has a single seat for two riders and is open. There's little privacy in these buggies. It's meant to be intimate but yet is open to discourage certain unsuitable behavior."

"I like the idea of the courting buggy. It sounds very romantic. Sorta like an open carriage ride in New York City." Violet left out a deep breath. "Nick's home is in New York. I'd love to be in a carriage with him."

Her cousin was absolutely right. Being in Samuel's courting buggy was romantic. Telling Violet about their dating customs made her realize how special dating was in the Amish faith. It seemed much better than going to college to meet new people. Of course, young adults in the English world went mainly to college for the purpose of furthering their education, not to find a mate. She didn't have any desire to go for higher learning, but she knew Judith sometimes wanted to go to high school to learn more. Judith had self-educated herself with all the books she read. Their mother had been frustrated on more than one occasion with Judith when she needed to do her chores, but was instead buried in one of her many books.

Aunt Carrie slid the glass door shut behind her and returned to the pool area. With her hands on her hips, she said, "Not good news, I'm afraid. Marlene's unhappy about the situation here. Apparently, Donna...the woman she has to keep an eye on this house told her nephew about our visit. He is short on cash so when Donna realized we were coming, she told him to come."

Violet's brown eyes widened. "I'm surprised that Marlene let it slip out about us being the visitors. You asked her to keep it quiet."

"She didn't mention our name and just said her friends, but I guess Donna remembered reading that we lived next door to Marlene. That's not hard to believe because Marlene's husband has been in pictures with your father many times." Aunt Carrie sat down. "Marlene's afraid she might have said that her neighbors were going to use her beach house, so that caused Donna to investigate further."

"Mom, we might approach Mr. Sullivan and give him a few pictures of us, so he won't take any when we aren't watching." Violet glanced at her. "We'll tell him not to take any of you."

"I'm sorry I talked to him." Rachel hoped her conversations with Mr. Sullivan hadn't made the situation worse for her relatives. She knew how they hated the media to exploit them while they were spending family time together.

Aunt Carrie patted her arm. "It's okay. He did tell you that he was a photographer, so he was blunt about his career. We probably don't have anything to worry about."

"Mom, I'm curious. Did an Amish guy ever take you home in his courting buggy before you met Dad?"

"*Ya*, a few times but nothing serious ever happened."

"It's hard for me to imagine you with anyone else except for Dad."

Aunt Carrie said, "Me too."

Rachel watched as Aunt Carrie resumed knitting. She'd been curious what her aunt was making. It looked like a blanket. "What are you knitting?"

"It's a prayer shawl. I started knitting a shawl for a good friend, Rose, who had to deal with cancer tests, chemotherapy, and other treatments." Aunt Carrie sighed, looking up from her knitting. "She never complained except to tell me she was cold all the time. I used to drive her to her appointments so I spent a lot of time in waiting rooms. I started knitting her a shawl. I prayed for Rose as I knitted it, because I wanted her to be covered in prayer when it was finished."

Rachel covered her legs with a beach towel. She felt refreshed from swimming but a bit chilled. "How's Rose doing?"

Aunt Carrie stopped knitting for a moment. "She didn't make it."

"Mom started a prayer shawl ministry at our hospital back home." Violet smeared sunblock on her exposed body. "The ministry is popular with the nurses. They told mom that they want to take care of the whole person—physically, emotionally and spiritually."

Aunt Carrie said with pride, "Violet has knitted a few prayer shawls too."

"That's so wonderful you have this ministry. *Mamm* never mentioned it to me."

"She probably didn't because I had started it shortly before she passed on. We planned on getting together so I could give her my prayer shawl instructions. We were going to shop and get yarn on my next visit."

I should help with this project. I can imagine hearing my mamm's voice encouraging me to knit shawls for cancer patients. Doing something her *mamm* had wanted to do would give a sense of unity and closeness with her. "I'd like to help and knit shawls. How long does it take to knit one?"

"Each shawl takes about fifteen hours." Aunt Carrie tucked a stray lock of hair back into her knot. "You could even help me finish this one. We can together pray many blessings into this shawl."

"That sounds *wunderbaar, Aenti.* I like that we can work on the shawl together." *I should write Judith and tell her about the prayer shawls. I wonder how she's doing in cooking the family's breakfasts and suppers. Was Judith able to get the boys' lunches packed in time each morning?*

Her *daed* said he could fix his own lunch. It'd be nice to call Judith and see how they were doing without her. Maybe she'd call once on Violet's phone while Judith was at school. They had a phone in a shanty outside the schoolhouse for emergencies.

As she watched Violet put the chair down and stretch out on it, her thoughts returned to Samuel. Leaning back on her own chair, she removed her sunglasses and closed her eyes. The sun's rays felt soothing. Was Samuel able to get his orders filled? He worked hard and was a fine Amish man. *I bet while I'm away, Mary Zook will take him food.* At Sunday sings, she'd noticed Mary eyeballing Samuel with interest, but he'd never seemed to notice this attention. But would he while she wasn't there? *I don't like thinking about Mary trying to weasel her way into Samuel's heart while I'm gone. Mary is pretty with her strawberry blond hair and she's outgoing.*

She knew one thing, for certain. She missed Samuel, more than she thought possible. And she hoped Mary Zook wasn't a great pie maker. Samuel had a weak spot for butterscotch pie.

CHAPTER TWELVE

Samuel looked up after finishing taking a phone order from a customer when he saw Matthew and Noah walk into his store. Both boys looked presentable in their neatly pressed black pants with blue shirts so Judith and Rachel's father must be keeping these two in line. He grinned at them and asked, "Are you in the right store? Katie told me you've visited the bakery after school."

"We've stopped in for a snack yesterday before going home," Matthew said. "Rachel's cookies are almost gone. But today we need to talk to you about something important."

Noah said, "We've been studying dolphins in school—"

"And we worked hard on our reports." Matthew continued, "So we'd like to see a dolphin in person."

Samuel rubbed his chin. "I suppose you could go see dolphins at the Cincinnati Zoo. But I'm not sure they have any there."

Noah shook his head. "I asked Judith and she said no sharks or dolphins are at the Cincinnati Zoo. But that's okay, it'll be better to see dolphins that jump out of the ocean water where Rachel is."

"Are you going to see Rachel in Florida?" Matthew pleaded, "Please say yes. We want to go with you. We just have to see dolphins."

"We want to ride a dolphin too," Noah said. "We think Uncle Scott could arrange for us to do that."

"I'm sorry but I'm not going to Florida. This is Rachel's special time to relax and to enjoy spending time with your English relatives." He smiled at them. "She might not appreciate seeing all three of us in Florida. But I agree it would be great to see real dolphins playing in the ocean water. I bet you'll get a chance sometime. I'm sure that Aunt Carrie will be happy to have you visit in the future, but now isn't a good time."

Matthew rolled his eyes. "But we want to see Rachel now. She might forget us and not come home. She hasn't sent us a postcard even. She said she would."

"I'm sure she sent you a postcard. It's too soon to receive one from her. I haven't received one either, but I know it'll take a few days to get here. Florida's mighty far. It took them probably around fourteen hours of driving to get there," Samuel explained, hoping that would convince them why they shouldn't expect to get mail yet from Rachel.

With intense frustration in his voice, Noah said, "Don't you miss Rachel? She's going to be there for a long time. We miss her a lot."

Matthew nodded vigorously in agreement. "It's been hard not seeing Rachel every day. We need to see her."

Samuel nodded. "I do miss Rachel but I'm still not going to Florida. She hasn't been gone long. And I don't think your father would want you two to go even if I did get a ride to Florida. Cocoa Beach is miles away from here. It would take hours and hours to get there."

Matthew shrugged. "*Daed* won't care if we go. He says all the time we wear him out. I think he needs a break from us."

"You'd be doing him a big favor," Noah said.

He crossed his arms. "I'm sure he won't want you to leave right now. He won't want you to miss any school."

"Well, if you change your mind," Mathew said, "let us know."

"*Ya*, you know where to find us," Noah said over his shoulder.

He stood and said, "Bye, boys. Sorry I couldn't help you but I'm sure Rachel's thinking about you both and will bring something home for you. Maybe seashells or some kind of a souvenir." He watched them hop on their scooters outside his shop. He shook his head, thinking how the boys thought it'd be simple to get a ride to Florida. Must be nice to be young enough to think it was possible to drop everything and get a ride to see dolphins. *But I do wish I could go to Florida and see Rachel. I wonder when she'll get my letter.*

After the boys left, he walked to an unfinished headboard that needed to be painted white. The customer loved white furniture and she wanted him to paint all their bedroom pieces white. He'd probably stay tonight and do the painting after he closed the store.

At the sound of his sister Katie's voice, he turned around to greet her. "I'm getting all kinds of visitors today. Rachel's brothers were just here."

"They mentioned they needed to see you before they started for home. Something about dolphins." Katie briefly touched the piece of bed furniture. "I'll probably never need one of your lovely headboards."

His poor sister. She loved Tim but he didn't think a marriage between those two would happen now. He'd seen Tim himself with the non-Amish young woman, and they looked happy together. "Have you talked with Tim lately?"

"Tim's definitely interested in the English woman. He came to see me today during lunch to tell me he was becoming serious about her." Katie's lower lip trembled and her blue eyes glistened with tears. "It's definitely over between us. I wouldn't be surprised if he gets married in the month I thought we would."

Samuel patted her shoulder. "I'm sorry, Katie. I know it hurts. Tim wasn't the right man for you. It's best to know it now before a marriage took place. God has someone else in mind for you."

"Maybe I put too much pressure on Tim to get married to me this fall and I pushed him into another relationship. I just don't see how he could already be serious about someone else."

"I don't think he's going to get married this year. He has to decide if he can marry a non-Amish woman. He's going to need time to decide if he loves her enough to leave his faith. He's accepted the rules of the *Ordnung* when he was baptized."

She frowned. "If he does leave our church, I hope he doesn't regret it later. He'll be shunned by his family."

"Have you heard from Rachel?"

"No, I haven't. Could I use your phone to call Rachel? I need to talk to my best friend. I'll give you money for the call. I don't want to use the phone in the bakery. I'm afraid Mary Zook will listen to my conversation." She smoothed her white apron. "Actually I'm sure she would. Samuel, don't be surprised if she tries to get you to take her home from work."

Mary had already been in his store a few times since Rachel left. She made him feel uncomfortable. His lunch time had even been intruded by Mary. He'd always closed the shop during his lunch time so he could eat at the bakery. Why in the world couldn't a man eat his lunch in private without Mary standing next to his table and chatting constantly? He might have to start packing his lunch so he wouldn't have to deal with Mary. He didn't want to be rude to her, but he wasn't going to court her. Rachel would be back soon or he hoped she would be.

"Thanks for the warning about Mary. She's been buzzing around me like a fly."

Katie smiled. "Except you can't swat her like you can a fly."

"I'm planning on leaving later tonight and paint that headboard, so I have an excuse ready for Mary."

"Hopefully, she won't offer to work late at the bakery, but I'm sure our mother won't allow it."

"Go ahead and call Rachel. You don't need to pay me. I'd like to talk with her after you're finished. Her Aunt Carrie's cell phone number is right on my desk by the phone." He wished he'd thought to call Rachel while the boys were here so they could talk to her.

"Thanks, Samuel." She took another glance at the headboard. "You do beautiful work."

"*Danki.*"

He wondered what Rachel would think of Tim and Katie's breakup. If Tim hadn't met this other woman, would things have been different for Katie? It was for the best that it happened now instead later. Obviously, Tim's feelings were not deep enough to marry Katie. But he knew, for sure, that his were for his beautiful Rachel.

Glancing toward the back of the room, he saw Katie speaking on the phone. She must have gotten a hold of Rachel. While waiting his turn to talk, he glanced at a copy of the Cincinnati Enquirer newspaper. A customer had left it because of an entertainment center they liked was shown in an ad and wanted him to build one just like it. He chuckled to himself when he saw a story about dolphins in the paper. That was something how Matthew and Noah mentioned wanting to see dolphins in Florida, and now there was an article about them in this paper. He'd have to ask Rachel if this was a sign he should visit Florida.

"Samuel, I'm done."

Quickly, he walked to his mammoth desk where he kept all his business papers, orders and phone. Katie stood, leaving his chair empty for him. "Hi, Rachel."

"Hi. It's *wunderbaar* to hear your voice."

"Your brothers were here this afternoon. They want to go to Florida to see dolphins and to see you. They asked me to go with them and arrange the ride."

"I miss those two. I'll call them sometime soon."

He heard a lot of voices in the background. "I guess you aren't at the beach house. I hear men talking."

"You hear Uncle Scott and Adam." Rachel paused for a moment. "And Adam's friend, Nick Foster. They just got here."

"I've heard Adam speak about his friend, Nick, but I didn't know he was going to the beach."

"I didn't know it until Adam asked Aunt Carrie if it was okay. They both came together because Nick flew his dad's plane."

He'd asked Adam to look out for Rachel. Instead, his friend Nick was there with Rachel. He didn't like the sound of this new development in Cocoa Beach. "It sounds like it'll be hard for you to make important decisions about your life with all these people there."

"Uncle Scott's leaving on Monday morning. I'm not sure how long Adam and Nick are staying. I think Nick wants to spend a little time with his father during spring break. His mother passed away a couple of months ago."

"Does he have any siblings?"

"No, he was an only child. It was sudden. His mother died in an automobile accident."

He decided to change the subject. "Has that photographer bothered you again?"

"No, but Aunt Carrie thinks he came here for the purpose of taking pictures of them. Uncle Scott's going to talk to Mr. Sullivan. He's going to tell him that he can have a couple of exclusive shots of him with Aunt Carrie, but only if Mr. Sullivan agrees that he won't take any unauthorized ones."

"That sounds like a good way to handle it." He cleared his throat. "I miss you, Rachel."

"I miss you too."

He heard someone call Rachel's name.

"I have to go. They want to play volleyball," she gave a short laugh, "and you know, I'm pretty good at it."

He didn't want to sound jealous but he had to know if she was playing volleyball with Nick. "You're an excellent player. Are the girls playing against the boys?"

"It's me, Violet and Nick against Aunt Carrie, Uncle Scott and Adam."

When he heard Nick was on Rachel's team, he was sorry he asked.

CHAPTER THIRTEEN

Rachel's escape to the heated pool refreshed her as she swam with deep strokes. She had been overjoyed to see Adam again, but uncomfortable about meeting Nick Foster.

There was no doubt in her mind how crazy Violet was about Nick. Her cousin's brown eyes lit up like the neighbors' Christmas tree with hundreds of lights on it. Violet's glowing eyes went unnoticed by Nick. He talked mostly to her, or rather tried to involve her in a conversation. Fortunately, Uncle Scott arrived shortly after they did, so Nick's attention to her was diverted.

Maybe she could stay out here until they went to bed. It was peaceful swimming by herself. It was rather nice not to be around people and to enjoy the quiet. Right now, Adam, Nick and Aunt Carrie went to watch a movie together, while Uncle Scott said he needed to talk with Violet about her summer job in his office. He thought it'd be a great experience for her to work for him. After several minutes of swimming, she decided to get out of the pool to enjoy the quiet of the night and spend time thanking God for his many blessings to her.

While her feet were still on the ladder rungs, she heard, "Hey, it's Nick. I'm sitting out here. I said something to you when I first came out, but I guess you didn't hear me."

She glanced around the pool until her eyes focused on Nick. Only a light in the pool itself illuminated the area with several color-changing shows. *How long had Nick been watching her swim,* she wondered. "Didn't you like the movie?"

"I felt restless so decided to go for a walk on the beach and thought I'd see if you'd like to join me. I could use some company."

"Well, I'm wet so it'll be too chilly for me. You might ask Violet." Why couldn't he spend time with Violet instead of seeking her out? She could see why Violet was attracted to Nick. To say he was good-looking wouldn't be a strong enough adjective in describing him. Violet would say that Nick was a hottie because of his charming smile, perfect facial features, and athletic body. Before meeting Nick, Violet mentioned to her how he resembled actor Michael Weatherly, who played Tony on one of her favorite television series. She'd watched an old episode of the action drama, NCIS, with Violet before Nick and Adam had arrived. Violet was right. Nick was a younger version of the actor. She pulled a towel off a chair and rubbed her limbs quickly before wrapping it around her body.

"She's still talking to her dad," Nick said.

Her Aunt Carrie had said that it might be a good thing for them to share their feelings about their mothers' deaths. Surely, she hadn't meant the very first night Nick arrived. They barely knew each other, but what could it hurt? Violet would understand and Nick seemed to want someone to walk with him. She could wear Aunt Carrie's cover-up dress over her suit while they walked on the beach. It might be better to go now because Nick wouldn't be able to see much of her. Instead of clothing covering her body, the dark night would.

"Okay, I'll walk with you." She put the towel down and picked up the cover-up.

"Here, let me help you."

Nick put the crochet dress over her head before she could refuse. Then he lightly touched her shoulder. She decided not to take offense at him touching her like this, and murmured, "*Danki.* I mean thank you." She edged quickly away from Nick. An Amish man would never have been this familiar with a woman, especially when first meeting her. *I wish I was wearing my dress and kapp.*

It better be a short walk, she thought as she slid her feet into flip flops. "Okay, I'm ready for our walk."

He stared at her for a moment. "Your long hair is beautiful."

"Thank you." She followed him down the steps to the beach, but uneasiness never left her as their feet touched the sand. She should have suggested they stayed by the pool and talked instead. Maybe Violet would've joined them. Okay, he just was being nice by commenting on her hair, but he seemed too personal to her.

She wasn't sure if Nick was aware that she was Amish. "Usually my hair's pinned up under a prayer covering. Violet talked me into wearing other clothes. Well, actually I wanted to try to wear English clothing on the beach too. It's been an adjustment not to have my normal Plain clothing on."

"Adam mentioned you're Amish and his mom was raised Amish. I'm afraid I don't know very much about this faith except that you travel in buggies instead of cars."

"We're Christians so have that in common with a lot of people. But are different in that we avoid many conveniences of modern technology."

"Other than the clothing, have you enjoyed experiencing new things?"

She nodded. "Pretty much."

"Are you warm enough?"

"I am."

He sighed. "One reason I wanted to come to the beach with Adam was because my mother loved the ocean. I'm from New York and we went to the beach a couple of times a year. I thought maybe I'd feel close to her here."

"Did you come to this beach with your mom?"

"We did come here a couple of times, but we went mostly to Myrtle Beach, Outer Banks, and Ocean City."

"This is the first time I've been to any beach. I always wanted to see the ocean." She paused for a moment. "I'm sorry about your mother. I lost mine too. It's been a year since she passed on."

He stopped walking and touched her arm. "I'm sorry for your loss too. It sucks everything out of you when you lose your mother. Everyone tells me that time heals. Has it for you?"

The pain in his voice struck her hard. Nick's honesty about his feelings gave her the courage to speak what was in her heart. "I haven't gotten over losing my *mamm*. We were close. She was only forty-four when she suddenly died from a heart attack. How old was yours?"

"Mom was forty-six. She was beautiful and full of life. She never complained about anything. It seems so unfair that someone like her was killed in an automobile accident. Just a tragic and senseless thing to happen."

"I feel the same way. I don't think my mom should've died at her age. She'll never see my brothers grow up and have had a chance to become a grandmother. She was looking forward to my brother and his wife starting a family. I think she would have survived her attack if she could have gotten medical care right away."

"How about we stop and sit on a sand dune? I'm leaving Sunday to spend time with my dad, so I might not get a chance to talk to you privately again about my mom."

She hoped Violet wouldn't miss them. Her Uncle Scott was probably still telling Violet more about her summer job. And how could she refuse Nick's request? Sadness filled his voice when he spoke about his mother. She understood how he felt. Maybe venting to each other would ease the pain a little. "Or we can sit on a bench that's at the top of those steps." She pointed to a spot under a light. "I sat there yesterday when I watched the waves. It was peaceful. And if people use the steps, there's plenty of room for them to walk by us."

"Sounds good."

They crossed the beach to the bench. He sat close to her but she didn't say anything. The bench was smaller than she remembered. At the whiff of his pleasant fragrance, she realized he wore men's cologne. Amish single men shaved but never splashed any cologne on after shaving.

He ran his fingers through his light brown hair. "The man who killed my mother was driving with an expired driver's license and had a few too many drinks. Why did he have to be driving drunk that night? Mom was on her way home after volunteering at the children's hospital."

"My grandparents were killed by a teenager using his cell phone while driving."

"That's awful." His gray eyes widened as he stared at her. "I remember now that Adam mentioned going to their funeral and how the media showed up to tape his dad being there."

She nodded. "They had their cameras filming us as we rode in our buggies. After my grandparents' funeral, *Mamm* complained about being tired. I figured she wasn't sleeping well because of losing both her parents suddenly. I tried to help her more with cooking and everything. I worked at a bakery in town but cut my hours some."

"How's your dad doing? Mine isn't doing well. I worry about him all the time."

"My dad's been sad and he misses her a lot."

"It's too bad that he didn't come with you to the beach. Maybe it would help him to get away. I'm going to tell my dad we should go away after my spring quarter ends. I don't have to start my summer job immediately."

She exhaled a deep breath. "There's been tension in our home between me and my dad. When Aunt Carrie invited me to spend time with her, I was glad to leave home. I haven't been able to make certain decisions, and also have always wanted to see the ocean. It seemed like a good thing to do."

"Does he expect too much from you?"

"I blame him for not putting a phone in our barn or building a shanty for a phone. See, the Amish don't believe in having phones in our houses, but our bishop allows us to have phones for emergencies and for business. We think family should spend time together instead of talking on the phone to others. Keeping the phone outside the house helps us to remember it's only to be used when necessary. When my mom had her heart attack, our English neighbors were on vacation so we couldn't use their phone. I think if we had been able to call for medical help right away, my mom might have lived."

"That has to be rough knowing having access to a phone nearby might have helped your mom to survive her attack." He squeezed her hand. "Did your dad put a phone in now?"

She shook her head. "He hasn't. My older brother Peter has a phone in his barn now so that might be why. It takes twenty minutes to get to his place, and we can use our English neighbors' phone when they are home. I have twin brothers, Matthew and Noah, who are ten and can be mischievous. Maybe he's afraid those two will use the phone if he puts one in now."

"I can't forgive the driver who killed my mother. I know I should but I feel a lot of anger at him."

"He had no business driving in his condition." She was quiet for a few minutes while watching the waves hit the beach. "It's not just the phone why I can't forgive my dad. My mom wanted him to take her to the doctor and he didn't. Of course, she could have gone herself but I think she must have been too tired to drive the buggy. I wish she had asked me. I didn't know about the pain she had but just thought she was tired."

"It's not your fault."

"That's what my boyfriend said."

"Adam mentioned being friends with Samuel. He said Samuel wants to marry you."

She grinned at Nick. "It sounds like you guys are as chatty as women."

He chuckled. "Well, I don't know about that. I suppose Samuel is Amish too."

"Yes and we have an understanding. We aren't engaged but are serious. Before my grandparents and *Mamm* died, I planned on joining the church and getting baptized so we could get married. I came here to get answers before I make any big decisions. Right after my mother's death, I quit my job and stayed home to take care of my family. I'm thankful that Aunt Carrie gave me this chance to come here. Being away from home will give me the perspective I need to decide what to do about my life. Or I hope so anyhow."

Turning his head, Nick looked directly into her eyes. "I'm glad you're here. I feel a connection to you, even though we just met. Unfortunately, we have both suffered a lot from losing loved ones. So where do we go from here?"

"What do you mean? I suppose we should go back to the house. We can't stay out here all night."

"I meant I'd like to stay in touch with you after I leave here on Sunday. I usually call and text friends but not sure how I can remain in contact with you. If you don't use a phone often, I'm sure you don't text people or send emails to friends."

Nick's question surprised her. How could she answer him? She couldn't bear to hurt his feelings but staying in touch with each other wasn't a good idea. Or was it? She might not join the church and marry Samuel. "God might just mean for us to vent our feelings to each other during this time. And we might not want to continue after this weekend. But we can decide later what to do if we want to stay in touch." She smiled at him. "By Sunday, you might be tired of me and that will be it."

"I seriously doubt that will happen. There's something about you that makes me want to get to know you better." His hand grasped hers. "I'd like to meet your family. Maybe I could visit you sometime this summer and experience Amish living. My home's in New York so it would just take a short time to fly to Fields Corner. I already checked the distance."

His intimacy wasn't appropriate. And Nick visiting in Fields Corner wasn't a good idea. Besides, Violet wanted Nick to be interested in her. *I better get back to the house quickly before Nick says something else that he shouldn't.* She didn't like the way he looked at her and was afraid of what he might say next. "Let's walk back. It's getting late and the others will be wondering what happened to us."

She stood and walked down the steps. Getting her Plain clothes out to wear tomorrow might be a good idea.

CHAPTER FOURTEEN

Kevin snapped a few more shots of them. What luck that Rachel and a young man were on the bench in front of his aunt's place. He'd gotten some fantastic shots with them sitting close. He couldn't wait to zoom in on their faces back at his aunt's. Hopefully, a romance would develop between the two. A non-Amish guy with an Amish woman. He had a feeling that the guy was definitely enamored of Rachel. His friend wanted to do a documentary about Amish teens going wild during *rumschpringe*. Beautiful and demure Rachel would be awesome for it, but he wasn't going to worry if it didn't happen. That might be pushing it, and she'd been pleasant to him about including her with his beach photos. Of course, she might not be as thrilled when his pictures were published, and she realized how many more he took of her.

Obviously, his pictures of an Amish girl would interest many people. There was a big interest in anything

Amish. Over a year ago, he'd watched with great curios-
ity the TV coverage of the funeral procession for Carrie
Robinson's parents. There were many buggies following
the black, also horse-drawn hearse. Geez, it was hard to
imagine people driving buggies instead of cars and not
having electricity in their homes. No wonder there was
such a fascination with their unusual and simple lifestyle.

After he received a hefty paycheck for these pictures,
he'd be back on his feet. Maybe he'd purchase an Amish
quilt for his ex. When they were married, Tammy mentioned seeing a handmade bedspread that was beautiful
but expensive. He probably should have bought it for her
for an anniversary present, but he'd never been very
good in the gift buying department. Thinking about his
ex-wife wasn't a good thing, because now depression
pulled at him. He'd been lonely for a long time... ever
since the divorce.

Only problem was what happened between him and
his aunt today. She blew up at him and told him to stop
taking pictures. She was upset that the owner Marlene
called to see if she had intentionally told him about the
Robinson family visiting. Aunt Donna liked Marlene and
enjoyed taking care of the beach house for her. When
Marlene mentioned her neighbor was going to use their
place, Aunt Donna mentioned to him that it had to be
Carrie Robinson coming with her daughter and niece.
She remembered a prayer shawl Marlene had knitted
while staying at the beach and telling her how Carrie
Robinson started the ministry of giving shawls to cancer
patients. Marlene had gone on and said how Carrie was

the best neighbor. Apparently, Marlene felt that Carrie made a wonderful political wife, because she was sweet and supportive of her husband's aspirations, even though she was a private person. When Marlene told her to get groceries for three people, she'd figured out which neighbor was visiting. She'd been so excited that a senator's wife would be next door. Aunt Donna had even researched on the Internet everything about the Kentucky senator and his family.

Aunt Donna received a call from Carrie thanking her for the groceries. She'd been on cloud nine talking with a famous senator's wife. His aunt had to know he would take pictures. She knew it was his job and only source of income. After all, his aunt was the one telling him to visit because the Robinsons would be vacationing next door.

He knew what had to be done... contacting the news media about his pictures. And soon.

* * *

After she entered her bedroom, Rachel's breathing slowed to a normal rate. She'd enjoyed talking with Nick about their mothers, but his comments about wanting to get to know her better and staying in touch alarmed her. She should stick close to Violet tomorrow, so Nick would have to spend time with both of them.

While she removed her nightgown from a drawer, Violet knocked once and asked, "Is it okay I come in?"

She turned toward the door and said, "*Ya*, please do."

Violet's brown eyes stared directly at her. "Well, I was right, wasn't I?"

"About what?"

"That Nick would probably become interested in you." Violet sat on the edge of the bed. "I heard you two went for a walk on the beach. I was hoping he'd ask me. I knew he'd fall for you. I saw the way he looked at you while we played volleyball."

"I was in the pool when he decided to go on a walk. He asked me because you were busy with your dad about your summer job. And Nick said he'd already seen the movie your *mamm* and *bruder* chose to watch. It was a short walk and we talked about losing our mothers."

"Did he talk about me?"

She shook her head. "We mainly talked about our sadness at our mothers dying suddenly. They were both only in their forties." Reassuring Violet was important because she didn't want jealously over Nick to come between them. "Don't worry. There's tomorrow and Saturday. I'm sure you'll get a chance to spend time with Nick."

Violet frowned. "I wish I played golf. The guys are going golfing tomorrow morning."

"It's nice that Nick's also working for your dad this summer. You'll get to spend time with him. He'll see you in a new light and not just as Adam's little sister."

"I hope so. I just love how his eyes crinkle at the corners. And his smile does crazy things to my insides." Her voice dropped. "I just wish Nick looked at me the way he did at you today."

She understood but didn't know what to tell Violet immediately. After sitting on the bed beside Violet, she squeezed her shoulder. "I hope he does too. I think when you least expect it, he'll ask you out. You're pretty, sweet, and a lot of fun. He'd have to be crazy not to notice you."

Violet grinned at her. "I might have a chance this summer when you and Adam aren't around."

"Do you think it'd be too weird for me to wear my own clothing tomorrow?" She fingered her nightgown, anxious to get out of her English clothes.

"Why do you want to do that?"

I don't want to tell Violet that Nick complimented my hair. It'd hurt Violet's feelings to know that he noticed my hair. If I wear a kapp and maybe a bonnet, too, Nick won't see my hair again. The English clothes are too revealing to wear around Nick, but the hair bothers me a lot. Only a husband someday should see my uncovered hair. She was taught this early that women shouldn't be the cause of distraction and shouldn't cut their hair. The Bible said that women should be discreet and modest when it comes to presenting themselves in public.

Glancing at Violet's jean capris and form-fitting top with her glorious hair cut to chin length, Rachel wondered briefly if life would be easier to be English. *Did Aunt Carrie have doubts before meeting Scott Robinson about joining the church?* Maybe her *mamm* had been wrong in saying her sister would've joined the church if she hadn't met Scott Robinson. He might have given her the courage to leave their Amish faith, but the thought could've already been in Aunt Carrie's head.

She shrugged. "What if you suddenly wore Plain clothing instead of your usual clothing? Wouldn't it seem strange to you? I thought I'd feel freer not wearing my dress, apron, and kapp... but I haven't. And I wanted to blend in with everyone else here by wearing non-Amish clothing."

"It'd be weird for me to dress Amish. I doubt I could handle the straight pins even." Then Violet gave her a disappointed look. "But you haven't worn all the clothes we bought."

"Maybe when the guys leave, I'll wear them." She sighed. "Okay, I'll tell you what else bothers me about not wearing my own clothing. I feel uncomfortable around the guys." *How can I explain without hurting Violet's feelings?* "It's just the way I was raised from a tiny girl. Remember when you were little and visited, you asked me why I dressed like Laura Ingalls from your book, *Little House on the Prairie.* My *mamm* heard your question and explained to you that Amish reject fads and fashion by wearing Plain clothing. It's also eliminates jealousy because everyone wears identical clothing so it promotes unity among Amish people. And wearing simple clothing makes it easier and shows our modesty as women."

Violet expression became thoughtful. "I miss Aunt Irene. She made me feel so special. Some adults talk down to children but she never did. I loved spending time with her and your family. One of the best weeks I had was when Mom and I stayed at your house when Adam, Peter and our dads went camping. I didn't miss not having television or electricity. It was an adventure and fun."

"It was great having just us girls together. The twins hadn't been born yet." Her eyes filled with tears. "Remember how our mothers worked on a quilt together while we played. I wish *Mamm* was here with us now."

Violet put her arm around her shoulders. "Those two sisters were close. My mom called to talk to your mom once a month."

She sniffed, then said, "I didn't know that."

"Your mom went to the neighbor's house to use their phone."

"*Mamm* said it was a blessing to have a sister. I'm glad they stayed close in spite of everything."

"I always wanted a sister. You and Judith seem close."

She nodded. "Judith and Katie want all of us to join the church together. I need to decide soon so I can start instructions. Judith and Katie have already talked with the bishop about joining in the fall."

"It's a big decision. I asked Mom once if she had joined the church before meeting Dad if she thought Aunt Irene would have shunned her." Violet frowned. "I don't get the whole shunning thing."

What would Mamm had done if circumstances had been different? She couldn't imagine her mother not having contact with her only sister. "What did Aunt Carrie say?"

"Mom said it was a good thing she met Dad first, but she thought Aunt Irene would've still somehow been part of our lives." Violet paused for a second. "But maybe she wouldn't have married Dad if she'd already been a church member. I've noticed how sad Mom is when she returns home after visiting all of you in Fields Corner. Deep down, I think she misses some aspects of the Plain life. It must be hard to be raised in a certain way of life that is totally different from what you switch to as an adult."

Rachel nodded. "I'm sure it must be, but I'm glad you're my cousin. I can't imagine you not being part of my life." She stood. "If we're getting up early to see the sunrise, we better get to bed."

"I'm definitely getting up. It'll be great to enjoy the beach when it's almost deserted."

"*Ya.* I hope Mr. Sullivan sleeps in."

"I don't think Dad has had a chance to speak to him. If Sullivan's on the beach, I'll tell him that Dad wants to speak with him about something important. I still can't believe a photographer has to be here during our time on the beach."

She was glad that he had only taken pictures of her wearing Plain clothing.

After Violet left the room, she started getting ready for bed. After she was dressed in her nightgown, she went into the adjoining bathroom and thought how nice it was to have this privacy. They only had one bathroom in their house, but appreciated they had indoor plumbing. Not all Amish had this convenience and used outside bathrooms.

While brushing her teeth, she recalled Violet's question about why she wanted to wear her Plain clothing tomorrow. She could've said much more, and how dressing alike in simple clothing helped to avoid envy and jealousy which the Amish wanted to avoid. These emotions might break down a community and also cause sin.

"Thou shalt not covet," was a commandment they tried to follow on a daily basis.

She'd noticed in the outside world, modesty wasn't always an issue among both men and women. Unfortunately, it seemed like some non-Amish individuals revealed as much as possible sometimes. *But I couldn't say that to Violet. It sounds judgmental and that's a sin too.*

Replacing her toothbrush in the traveling case, she thought how her *mamm* called Aunt Carrie every month. Then she thought how Nick's mother was only forty-six when she died. If her mother had been killed in an automobile accident, would it have been easier to accept? Would she have been able to move on with her life by now? Her bitterness might have been focused on the driver instead of her *daed.* Deep in her heart, she'd forgiven the young driver who killed her grandparents. It'd been a hard thing to do, but she'd been raised to forgive others for their mistakes, even when they were careless enough to kill someone. Following Jesus meant doing what He said in the Lord's Prayer: "Forgive us our trespasses as we forgive our trespassers."

She knew God forgave her for past and present sins, so extending forgiveness to her *daed* was something she needed to work on. *Obviously God doesn't want me to have a hardened heart against Daed for being too cheap to install a phone and for not being sensitive to her mamm's failing health. And Nick needs to forgive the driver who took his mother's life.*

One thing she needed to remember was her *mamm* was in heaven. *I need to accept that it was apparently her time to die.*

After she kneeled by her bed, Rachel prayed, "Loving Lord, You gave the gift of forgiving others to your son Jesus, even when he was hurt and betrayed. Help me to be able to forgive others, especially my *daed*. I don't want to feel this bitterness toward him any longer. It's been a burden that I've placed on myself. I've been wrong to blame my father. Please open my heart to be loving and forgiving."

CHAPTER FIFTEEN

"Would you stop laughing?" Rachel tried to give Violet a stern look.

Between giggles, Violet said, "I'm sorry. I never expected to see you wearing your Plain clothes with flip flops."

"It'd be sillier for me to wear my black shoes and socks while walking on the sandy beach."

"That's true."

"I could go barefoot. I go barefoot a lot at home. Wearing my Amish clothing feels right to me." She eyed Violet's clothes, noticing the pink blouse with dark jean capris. "I like what you have on. You look pretty in pink."

"Pretty enough to get Nick's attention?"

"Definitely." Rachel stopped walking to gaze at the sunrise. "It's peaceful and beautiful this morning."

A young couple, holding hands, walked toward them. Violet nudged her side. "I wonder if they want to take your picture."

"I hope not, but since I'm not a baptized member of the church, it won't be as bad to have my picture taken. I didn't tell Mr. Sullivan that, because I didn't want to encourage him in taking our pictures because it would be wrong for me to pose for any picture. But he took the pictures of the ocean which I happened to be in, and he didn't ask me to pose so that was good."

"I didn't know your picture can be taken since you're not baptized. I want a picture of you." Violet grinned. "Or I'll have Mom snap a candid one of us together but we won't pose."

She shrugged. "In our district pictures of children are allowed if the whole face doesn't show. So it seems that there's a more lenient view of photography in some instances, but definitely not if you're baptized. "

When the couple was only a couple of feet away, they smiled and said, "Hello."

The woman's auburn hair was short and curly. She wore turquoise earrings that matched her blouse. She asked Violet, "Would you mind taking a picture? We're on our honeymoon and want to get a picture of us on the beach together."

"Congratulations on your wedding. I'll be happy to take your picture."

The woman handed a small digital camera to Violet. "Thank you. We appreciate it."

Violet snapped several pictures before giving the camera back to the new wife. "Look at what I took and if you want me to take more, I will."

After glancing at the pictures, the wife, said, "They're perfect."

While her husband looked at the pictures, the wife asked Rachel, "Are you Amish? The reason I ask is because my cousin is Amish. She lives in Ohio. Well, actually my mother was raised Amish but she's not now."

Rachel nodded. "I'm Amish. I'm from southern Ohio. Where does your cousin live?"

"Mary lives in Fields Corner. She just started working at a bakery and loves it."

The husband grinned. "Mary likes her job because she's interested in the guy next to the bakery. He has a furniture store, and we bought a headboard from him."

"It's gorgeous. I'm glad we went to Weaver's Furniture store while we visited Mary. We're thinking of buying more furniture from him."

She swallowed hard; surprised that Violet for once was quiet. "It's a small world. I'm from Fields Corner and I'm assuming your cousin is Mary Zook. I worked in Weaver's Bakery until my *mamm* passed on. And..." her voice trailed off because she wasn't sure whether to tell Mary's relatives that Samuel was her boyfriend.

"Rachel, here is my cousin and she's been dating Samuel Weaver for two years." Violet narrowed her eyes at the couple. "In fact, he's asked her to marry him."

Embarrassment crossed the wife's face. "I'm sorry. I didn't know. And here I'm blabbing about my cousin and you're from the same town."

"It's funny how you can travel a long distance and happen to run into someone from your area. We live in northern Ohio, but once we ran into a friend in New York at a Broadway play." The husband dropped the camera in his wife's beach bag. "Thanks for taking the pictures."

"We better scoot. We're going to breakfast. It was nice meeting you," the wife said in a rush.

"Bye. Enjoy your breakfast," Violet said. When they were out of hearing range, Violet turned to her. "Well, say something."

"I can't believe Katie never told me Mary was working at the bakery. She likes to bake but I'm sure the husband was right, and the main reason she's working there is because of Samuel. I've seen her looking at him whenever we're together."

"I wonder how fast Mary will get a call from her cousin. She looked shocked when I told her about you and Samuel. I'm glad I mentioned how long you two had dated. Mary needs to face it. She doesn't have a chance with Samuel."

Rachel gave a small laugh. "Can you believe it? I come all the way to Florida to get away from Fields Corner, and I run into relatives of Mary Zook's. She's never been my favorite person. I've been nice to her but she seems to dislike me."

"She's probably jealous of you. If I were Amish, I'd be chasing Samuel. He's a hottie."

"Is that right?" She decided to tease Violet. "I guess you want me to marry Samuel so you can get a discount on his furniture."

"Hey, that's a great idea. I saw a roll top desk I love on the Weaver's website." Violet turned and over her shoulder said, "Let's head back and eat breakfast. Walking has made me hungry."

Fifteen minutes later, they were seated at the table with plates filled with French toast, scrambled eggs, sausage, bacon and fruit. Aunt Carrie placed the coffeepot in the middle of the table before she joined them.

"Mrs. Robinson, everything looks delicious," Nick said as he broke off a piece of toast.

Rachel removed her black bonnet but kept her white *kapp* on her head. She saw Nick staring at her head. *I hope he doesn't ask why my hair's pinned up.*

"Thank you." Aunt Carrie smiled at Nick. "I want you boys to have enough energy on the golf course."

"Honey, you outdid yourself." Uncle Scott took a sip of his coffee. "And you make the best coffee."

Violet frowned. "Geez, Nick, why do you keep staring at Rachel's head?"

"I'm sorry. I'm a journalism major so I tend to be nosy. I was wondering about Rachel's black bonnet. Since we just talked about our mothers last night, the black bonnet reminded me of my mother's funeral."

Quickly, she swallowed her mouthful of sausage. "Single women wear black bonnets when going to town or other public places. And what I have on now is my prayer covering and is called a kapp."

With an amused expression, Uncle Scott said, "When I met my lovely wife here, I asked her the same question about her bonnet."

"You were a pest," Aunt Carrie said, fondly.

"Violet, it looks like we're going to have the same boss this summer," Nick said.

Adam groaned. "Dad, what were you thinking? You'll have your hands full with these two chatty ones."

"Oh, you're just jealous." Violet waved her fork at Adam.

Nick grinned at Violet. "Hey, we'll have to be lunch buddies."

She noticed how Violet's eyes brightened at Nick's statement. She was happy for Violet that Nick finally singled her out. Maybe it was God's plan for Nick and Violet to get to know each other better through their summer jobs.

* * *

"Adam, you and Nick put the golf clubs in the SUV while your dad has a second cup of coffee," Carrie said.

"Sure, Mom," Adam answered.

Rachel said, "Violet and I'll take care of the dirty dishes. Thank you for cooking breakfast. Everything was so good."

"Thank you," Carrie said as the girls picked up the plates and silverware from the table.

"This is nice having all of us together." Scott poured cream into his coffee.

"If Mr. Sullivan doesn't return your call about taking pictures and especially of Rachel, you need to try again. I didn't like how he happened to be around when Rachel went for walks. Even one morning when she got up early to walk, he was on the beach and asked her a lot of questions. He also stared at our cottage one day. That was creepy."

Last night the neighbor had given Scott her nephew's cell phone number. She'd apologized to Scott and mentioned her nephew wouldn't sell any pictures. However, Carrie still felt nervous that Sullivan might decide to profit off his pictures of Rachel. She'd hate if David decided her life was too worldly and wouldn't allow future visits with her nieces and nephews. Even though, Rachel hadn't posed for any, David wouldn't like to hear that pictures of his daughter were posted for the world to see. It couldn't be a coincidence that a photographer happened to visit his aunt during their spring break.

"I'll call him again this morning."

"Thanks, honey." She hated to tell Scott that if he wanted to play golf early in the morning, he better leave. She loved him being close to her again. Whenever he was away in D.C., she missed him and wished he had a different job. She patted his arm. "I like you being here but I suppose you better get a move on. I know how much you enjoy playing golf."

With a serious expression, Scott asked, "Has it been difficult talking about Amish customs? Do you have regrets?"

"I don't regret marrying you. I do wish I saw you more."

Leaning closer to her, his lips brushed hers with a sweet kiss. "I love you."

She smiled. "I love you more."

"I don't think that's possible. I give thanks to God daily for the day I happened to meet you."

She laughed. "It was a memorable meeting. You were in such a hurry that you ran into me and knocked my bags out of my hands."

He grinned. "I'm glad I made such a great first impression."

"I never expected a guy the size of a linebacker to run into me. You definitely got my attention." Her broad-shouldered guy could be a softie at times but other times, he fought hard for bills he believed should be passed.

Mr. Sullivan better return Scott's call soon, or else he might have to deal with her husband's ire.

* * *

Rachel set a bowl of fresh fruit salad on the table for lunch. Subs were on a big platter and Aunt Carrie put pitchers of iced tea and lemonade next to brightly colored blue and red glasses. She glanced at the arrangement and thought how the fruit and dinnerware looked colorful against the white table. Paintings of the beach with lighthouses and sand dunes were lovely against the white walls.

Nick whispered to Rachel, "How about we go outside to eat by the pool? I'd like to talk again. I kept having dreams last night about my mother."

After she glanced and saw Violet talking on her cell phone, Rachel nodded. "Sure."

Once seated at the glass topped round table, Nick said, "My mom looked younger in my dreams and happy. My dad and I were in a boat with her. We used to go boating a lot in the summers. It was lots of fun."

"That's good you have happy memories."

"I was hoping to have more. When I first woke up this morning, I'd forgotten she was gone. Did that ever happen to you?"

"Yes, at first, I expected to see my *mamm* in the kitchen. It was hard being in places where she used to be the most." She decided to go ahead and spill what she felt God wanted her to do about her father. "Last night, I realized I need to stop blaming my *daed* for not getting a phone and not taking *Mamm* to the doctor. I haven't wanted to forgive him but it's important I do." Should she suggest Nick do the same and forgive the driver who killed his mother? But it might be too soon to suggest it.

Nick's eyes filled with understanding. "You think I need to forgive the driver, don't you? But I don't think I can ever do that. He shouldn't have been behind a wheel."

"I understand. You need more time before your heart's ready to forgive. By the way, forgiving someone doesn't mean you forget what he did."

"I've heard forgiveness is a big thing in your faith."

"It is. Jesus teaches us to forgive and to realize God can bring good out of any tragic situation. Love and compassion toward others is what we're taught to do. I held on too long to blaming my father for my *mamm's* death. My grudge against my *daed* was wrong. Coming here and away from home has helped. I've gotten a new perspective about everything."

"That's great your attitude has changed toward your father. I'm sure he's a wonderful man. After all, he raised a pretty terrific daughter."

She swallowed a potato chip, then replied, "Thank you."

Nick took a bite of his meat sandwich and appeared to be deep in thought. "If you met the right guy, would you consider leaving your Amish community, like your Aunt Carrie did?"

This was the perfect opportunity to be clear about her feelings about Samuel. "I doubt I would for any man because I love my Amish boyfriend. If I marry anyone, it will be Samuel. Before I came here, I questioned what was right for me. I thought if my *mamm* had been English, she'd still be alive. Now, I'm thinking it might not have made any difference. God's way is best, even though it's hard to accept and understand at times."

"Maybe God wants you to experience a non-Amish life after leaving the beach. If you stay with your Aunt Carrie, I can visit and show you what the world has to offer. I respect your Amish upbringing because it's molded you into the person you are now, but I think it'd be great for

182 / D<small>IANE</small> C<small>RAVER</small>

you to expand your outlook and see what you're missing by being shut off from the real world."

She laughed. "I don't live in a sheltered spot. I come into contact all the time with outsiders or non-Amish people. When I worked in a bakery, I waited on tourists. Guess what? I shop at Wal-Mart. Isn't that where lots of Americans buy all kinds of items?"

"It's hard for me to imagine not having electricity. You can't enjoy watching TV or movies. I mean, what do Amish do for fun?"

Sipping iced tea gave her a moment to think how to reply to Nick's assumption that Amish couldn't entertain themselves without electricity. "We do lots of things. For example, we might go boating in the summers."

Nick gave her a glance of utter disbelief. "How in the world do you go boating? Do you get a non-Amish driver to haul the boat for you?"

She shook her head. "We use our buggies to haul light boats. Fishing is a popular pastime. I love to go fishing. My *daed* and oldest brother, Peter, like to go hunting. If the fishing and hunting trips are successful, then we have food for the family. Other outdoor activities are camping and bird-watching. My twin brothers, Noah and Matthew, like to keep lists of birds spotted on the farm." She chuckled. "That's one of the few times they're quiet."

"It sounds like you enjoy the outdoors."

She nodded. "We do spend lots of time outdoors be-cause we appreciate the beautiful scenery that God's blessed us with. I have to admit I have enjoyed a change of scenery. I'll never forget the beauty of the ocean and watching the waves hit the shore."

"I should take you for a plane ride. You'd love how everything looks so small from the sky."

"Thank you. That's a kind offer but I don't want to fly. We never go in planes unless there's a big emergency when it might be necessary." He looked disappointed so she decided to mention something else her family liked doing. Pointing a finger at him, she said, "Don't laugh but we work on huge puzzles in the winter. We read and play games together in the evenings as a family. We also enjoy ping pong and my brothers like playing basketball."

"What about teenagers? Don't they get bored?"

"We have what is called 'Sunday sings' and on these evenings, we socialize with other young people. The purpose is to meet the person we might marry someday. We might play volleyball with mixed teams of boys and girls. Or we might play some other outdoor game and of course, sing sometime during the evening. A supper meal is served around five o'clock and snacks are served before everyone goes home."

"I'd like to go to a Sunday singing. Would that be possible?"

Samuel might not like Nick arriving at a Sunday singing. *Well, just because Nick asked, doesn't mean he'd actually show up for an Amish social gathering.* "Sure. The ages range from around sixteen to into the twenties."

Nick smiled at her. "Thanks for answering my questions. Just one more question, if you don't mind. It's hard for me to believe that you don't use electricity. Don't you sometimes wish you could get your work done quicker by having electricity? You'd have more time to pray because your work would take less time to do with electricity."

She shook her head. "While doing work slowly, we have time to focus on what God's given us and there's more time to pray while working. And we do have gas power. Bottled gas is used to operate water heaters, stoves and refrigerators. We use gas-pressured lamps and lanterns to light homes, barns and shops. We have indoor plumbing. Our bishop in our church district allows the use of phones in our businesses. We can also have a phone in a shanty or in a barn so we remember that the phone is only to be used when necessary."

"Is there some way I can call you? Are you allowed a cell phone for emergencies?"

Was he interested in her or did he just want to learn more about the Amish in general? Nick was a journalism major so some of his questions might be so he could write a paper about their lifestyle. She grinned. "Are you writing an article about the Amish?"

"I happen to be interested in a beautiful Amish woman." He reached over and tugged on her kapp string. "I know why you switched to your Amish clothing, but it has made me even more aware of you. Your green dress shows off your gorgeous green eyes."

Nick caught on to one of the reasons I'm wearing my Amish dress. He's perceptive. I guess wearing my Plain clothing didn't get the result I wanted. Nick's still flirting with me. Not a good thing at all. I'll try to ignore his compliments. "I don't have a cell phone, but Violet knows how to get a hold of me."

CHAPTER SIXTEEN

On Saturday afternoon, Rachel sat on a chair in her bedroom to read Samuel's letter in private. After ripping open the envelope, she removed the sheet of notebook paper and read:

Dear Rachel,

I enjoyed talking to you this evening. I'm glad you, Aunt Carrie, and Violet arrived safely and are now in Florida. It's hard for me to believe you're so far away. I picture you running free and happy on the beach, feeling the ocean water on your feet, and your lovely green eyes filled with excitement. I'm glad you're having this opportunity to see and experience the joys of seeing the ocean for the first time.

While you're away I'll stay busy filling my furniture orders. Business has been good so I probably won't start building the house this spring. It can wait. If we should get married in the fall or winter (but I can wait until you're ready), we can live with your family for several months. It might be easier on your brothers. I know they are close to you. You're a fantastic sister to them.

This time apart has me realize even more how deeply I love you. I talked to Peter this evening, and he told me how I have plenty of time to get married. He also said I should enjoy being single. I need to learn to be patient. All good things are worth waiting for, and I can wait for as long as it takes for you to decide to marry me. If you choose not to marry me, it'll be difficult, but I'll have to trust God. Of course, I don't know why you wouldn't want to marry me someday. I'm kidding!

How is your rumschpringe going? Have you watched any movies or experienced anything that you won't be able to do once you join the church? This is a special time to share with your Aunt Carrie and Violet. I hope you enjoy your visit. Tell both of them I said Hi.

Well, I can't think of anything else to write except to say I love you, Rachel. The past two years have been wonderful for me because you and I have had many fun and memorable times together. Dating you has opened my eyes to how important it is to choose the right woman to be your helpmate. God blessed me when he brought us together. I hope our relationship continues to grow stronger in love and in faith.

Love,
Samuel

Samuel's letter warmed her heart. It was sweet of him to take time to write her a letter soon after they'd talked the first night she was here in Florida. She hadn't written him a letter yet, but she did write a message to him on a postcard. Samuel wrote many great things but she especially appreciated his thoughtfulness in suggesting they live with her family in the beginning of their marriage. Samuel making her brothers a priority touched a chord in her heart. Her brothers could be ornery but she loved them. It would also benefit Judith if she and Samuel lived for several months with the family. She knew that many times in an Amish marriage it was traditional for the couple to live at the home of the bride's parents until they were able to set up their own home the following spring. But originally Samuel had planned on their house being built in time for them to start their married life.

Samuel's such a considerate man. He's willing to making adjustments just to make me happy.

Although she loved being near the ocean, she already missed Samuel and her family. She loved the time spent with each little brother when she tucked them in at night. Her *mamm* used to tuck them in their beds, so she tried to fill this void for them.

Aunt Carrie stood in the doorway and said, "Rachel, Nick wants to say good-bye to you. His dad needs the plane so he's leaving soon."

Rachel slid her letter back into the envelope. "That's a surprise. He didn't get a chance to enjoy the beach very long. What's Adam going to do?"

"He's going to book a flight back to school." Aunt Carrie smiled. "How's Samuel?"

"He's busy as always but he took time to write me." She felt her cheeks getting warm. "Samuel said he'll wait for me."

"He's a smart man."

"I haven't had a chance to tell you that I can't continue to blame *Daed* for *Mamm's* death. I've been praying and realize I need to forgive *Daed* for not getting a phone. I'm sure *Daed* would've taken *Mamm* to the doctor if he'd known she had heart disease. Being away from home and having this free time without the daily routine of demands has given me time to look deeper inside myself and to pray. I've been too hard on *Daed.* I'm so glad you gave me this vacation, *Aenti.*"

Aunt Carried hugged her. "That's *gut.* Your *mamm* would be proud of you. Maybe you should give your *daed* a call today. We can call Peter and leave a message if he's not in the barn. I'm sure he won't mind getting your *daed* so you two can talk."

She liked Aunt Carrie's suggestion. "*Danki.* It'll be a relief to tell *Daed* my feelings.

* * *

"Judith, have you seen Noah and Matthew since lunch?" David Hershberger worried whenever too much time lapsed without seeing his twin sons. They were not like their older brother, Peter, and trouble seemed to find them. An active imagination might be useful at times in solving hard problems, but unfortunately their thinking processes could result in disaster.

He knew Judith had started sewing pants for the boys after lunch. They'd stood for her while she took their measurements. She'd mentioned new pants were needed for them because of their recent growth spurt. Maybe they had asked her permission to do something.

Judith stopped moving her feet on the sewing machine's treadle, and turned to look at him. "They said their chores were done and they were going to shoot basketballs."

Years ago, he'd put a basketball hoop on the side of the barn for Peter, and his youngest sons had recently acquired an interest in basketball. "I just came from the barn and they weren't there."

Judith glanced at the clock. "I lost track of time and you're right, it's been a few hours since I've seen them."

"Let's both search and make sure they aren't hiding somewhere here. If we don't find them, I'll call Peter. I didn't see their scooters in the barn so they might have hopped on them and went somewhere. But if they did that, why wouldn't they tell us?" He had a feeling Matthew and Noah were up to something and that's why they left without asking permission. But hopefully, they were not far.

Both rushed off to search inside the house and outside. While yelling their names, David was worried when he didn't hear any replies. *I've been too lax with my sons.* With Irene's sudden death and knowing that Rachel blamed him, it'd been a sad household. He hadn't done his duty as a father and kept better track of the boys. He'd depended on Rachel taking Irene's role as a mother and left the nurturing many times to her. Also Judith had stepped in doing a lot of the discipline when Matthew and Noah needed it. He shouldn't be surprised now that they hadn't taken the time to talk to him about their afternoon plans. But why hadn't they said anything to Judith?

He met Judith on the front porch. "Since their scooters are gone, they might have gone to Peter's. Let's go check the phone shanty and see if there's any message from Peter."

"That's a *wunderbaar* idea." Judith looked relieved. "I bet they went to see Peter. They did mention they wished there were cookies to eat. Maybe they went to see if Ella had cookies."

Within minutes, they were inside the small wooden building. He looked at the answering machine and said, "There aren't any messages. I'll call Peter and hope he's in the barn."

After a few rings, he heard Peter's voice. "Hi, Peter. Judith and I have looked all over and can't find Matthew and Noah. Are they there? Their scooters are missing."

"No, they haven't been here. Do you think they might have gone to see Samuel at the furniture store? I remember they mentioned they wanted him to help them build birdhouses."

"I suppose they might have ridden their scooters to his store." Realizing he didn't have a phone book or even a writing pad and pen to write Samuel's phone number down, he said to Peter, "Give Samuel a call. I hope they are there."

While he waited to hear back from Peter, he wondered again why Matthew and Noah left without saying anything to him or Judith. They knew better. *They aren't bad boys. Are they doing something that they couldn't ask permission for?*

* * *

Samuel glanced at the clock and saw it was three o'clock. He stretched his arms, deciding it was time to quit working and go home.

Before he locked up, his phone rang. He saw on the caller ID that it was Peter. Oh no, he hoped nothing was wrong. Peter seldom called him. What if Rachel had gotten injured while swimming in the ocean? What if she had been attacked by a shark? He picked up the receiver and said right away to Peter, "Is Rachel okay?"

"Did something happen to Rachel? We hadn't heard anything."

"We seldom talk on the phone so thought you might be calling to tell me that Rachel got injured." He exhaled a deep breath. "I'm glad it's not about Rachel. What's up then?"

"We have two missing boys. My *daed* and Judith are worried. Have you seen Matthew and Noah, by any chance?"

He ran fingers through his hair. "No, I haven't seen them today. The last time I saw them was on Thursday. They stopped in after school and wanted to know if I missed Rachel. They thought I should go to Florida to see her. Then the boys asked if they could go with me to see Rachel and the dolphins. They were pretty insistent about going and said your *daed* wouldn't miss them."

"That's interesting they want to go to Florida right now. What did you tell them?"

"I told them this was Rachel's time to relax and that I wasn't going to Florida. They were unhappy with my answer, and said to be sure to tell them if I changed my mind about traveling to Florida. I haven't seen them since."

"I wouldn't think they'd try to go to Florida on their own. They couldn't be that desperate to see Rachel and dolphins." Peter paused for a moment. "They did once get a Greyhound bus schedule because they wanted to go to a circus in Cincinnati. *Daed* and *Mamm* decided to take the whole family to the circus. I wonder if they got it into their heads to take a bus to Florida."

There wasn't a bus station in Fields Corner so Matthew and Noah would have to get a ride to one of the bigger towns to catch a bus to Florida. "But they'd have to get a ride to the bus station. I hope some stranger didn't give them a ride. I'll check around here in town and see if anyone has seen them. I'll call you back soon."

Samuel prayed silently that the boys were safe while he went next door to the bakery. Katie was putting a tray of sugar cookies in the display case by the register.

"Katie, have you seen Matthew and Noah? Peter just called and said the boys are missing."

She looked at him, after sliding the glass door shut. "I haven't seen them today, but they were here yesterday afternoon. They asked me if I had heard from Rachel and if she missed them. I told them I talked to Rachel but it was just about Tim. I reassured them that I was sure Rachel missed them."

"Did they mention to you how they wanted to go to Florida right now to see Rachel and to see dolphins?"

"They said something about wanting to go to Florida." She smiled. "They said you weren't a good boyfriend, and they couldn't talk you into taking them to see Rachel."

Mary Zook, carrying a pot of coffee, stopped by Samuel. "I saw Bishop Amos talking to them about fifteen minutes ago out front."

* * *

When Peter called him back to tell him the boys were recently seen in Fields Corner, relief flooded his body, but David's heart started beating fast again when he saw Amos' buggy with the boys drive past the shanty. "I have to go, Peter. Bishop Amos just brought the boys home. I'm glad they're home, but I can just imagine what he's going to tell me again."

"Sorry, *Daed*. I know you don't want to court the bishop's sister. I hope he doesn't pester you too much about her again."

Judith left the shanty first with David quickly following her to the house. Although he was happy to see that Matthew and Noah were okay, why did they go to Fields Corner in the first place?

"Thank you, for bringing the boys home," he said to Amos while his wayward sons took their scooters out of the buggy. For once, they were quiet.

"They were trying to figure out how to get to Florida to see their sister." Amos looked down at the boys standing outside the buggy. "I told them to talk to you the next time before they decide to run away."

"Matthew and Noah, go in the house. I'll be in soon." *I might as well get this conversation out of the way. I'm sure he wants to tell me that they need a mother.*

"David, this is serious. They're too dependent on Rachel. What if someone had given them a ride to the bus station?" Amos raised his eyebrows. "Anything could've happen to these two little boys trying to travel all the way to Florida to see a sister who just left a few days ago. I don't blame you and Judith, but I think an extra adult around might help."

"It's my fault for not realizing earlier that they were gone. It won't happen again.

Thanks again for bringing them home." *Should I remind Amos what we did once as boys?*

"I have a few more places to stop this afternoon. But please think about getting married again. Those boys need a mother. Bye, David." Amos slapped the reins.

Upon entering the house, he saw the twins and Judith sitting on chairs in the living room.

He gave each boy a hug before sitting down. "Okay, boys, you scared me and Judith. When we couldn't find you, we were worried and called Peter. He called Samuel to see if he'd seen you in town. Why would you think you could just leave your home and take off for Florida?"

"We wanted to go because we miss Rachel." Noah removed his straw hat and exhaled a deep breath.

Matthew said in frustration, "We thought it'd be a great chance to see dolphins with our sister."

Leaning forward in her chair, Judith said, "But she just left a few days ago."

David paced in front of the boys a few times, trying to absorb why his sons needed so desperately to see Rachel that they felt like leaving their home. "I miss Rachel, too, but it's her time to have a break from us. She has worked hard to keep us in clean clothes and food on the table." He glanced at Judith. "And Judith's been doing an outstanding job making sure all your needs are met."

"We love you, Judith, but we liked Rachel tucking us in at night." Matthew brushed a blond lock out of his eye. "She told us stories each night."

Judith looked hurt. "I read to you every night."

"We like it that you read to us. You're a great sister." Noah glanced at Matthew as if he was asking permission to continue. At Matthew's nod, he said, "Rachel tells us how much *Mamm* loved us and how happy she was in the hospital when we were born. She says that *Mamm* was thrilled to have twin boys. At our birth, *Mamm* said, 'God gave me two *wunderbaar* blessings' and Rachel said how overjoyed everyone was to see us."

"Rachel always asks us each night what was good about our day, just like *Mamm* used to." Matthew's blue eyes widened. "She asks if anything bad happened, too, and she's serious and wants to know stuff we do. It's nice to talk and have this special time with her."

"We know you have papers to grade, so we don't expect you to tell us all kinds of things like Rachel does." A thoughtful expression crossed Noah's face. "Right before bed and prayers, is a nice time to share. It's quiet and Rachel's the best listener."

David moved a chair closer to the boys to sit on. "I understand better why you were anxious to leave to see Rachel. I should've spent more time listening to you two. Losing your dear *mamm* suddenly has been hard on me, but I can see I should've shared my grief with you. I wanted to protect you, maybe, too much. Since I don't want this to happen again, I'm going to give you both an extra barn chore to do this week. What you did today was wrong."

Judith nodded. "Something bad could've happened to you. You are too young to travel by yourself that far. I'm happy you are back home and safe."

"We have to remember that it was God's will to take your mother. And He always knows best." Should he mention how Martha Weaver's cousin Susan just died suddenly, leaving ten children behind with the youngest one just an infant? They at least had Irene in their lives for a much longer time than some children had their mothers.

"Do you think Rachel will come home? We'll afraid she'll forget us and we won't see her again." Matthew's face scrunched up like he was ready to cry.

Noah patted his brother's knee. "Mattie, don't worry. We'll see her again. She might still marry Samuel. And he won't want to live in Florida."

Judith shook her head at them. "Rachel will come home to Fields Corner. She won't stay in Florida. Why in the world do you think she will?"

"She couldn't wait to see the ocean," Matthew answered. "I know she'll love the waves, the sandy beaches and the dolphins."

"Not the dolphins again," Judith mumbled. She smoothed her dark blue apron and said in a firm voice, "You know what? I'm going to take you to see dolphins sometime. I'm not sure when but I promise I will."

"I think we've had enough excitement for today, but maybe tomorrow we'll call Rachel so you two can talk to her." A thought crossed his mind about the boys' adventure. "Hey, what were you planning on doing with your scooters if you had managed to get to the bus station?"

"That was a problem but we decided to put them at the back of Samuel's furniture store, and have Aunt Carrie call you to get them for us."

David knew one thing he planned on doing that night. He'd spend time in the boys' bedroom and listen to them talk to him about their *mamm*, if they wanted. Or anything they needed to get off their chests was fine with him.

Apparently Rachel had filled roles of both mother and father. His eyes filled with tears. Her burden would be lighter when she came home. He would start spending time with his boys again. They hadn't been fishing since

Irene had passed on. They hadn't gone out on the boat last summer either.

This summer they would go boating too. It was time the Hershbergers enjoyed life again.

CHAPTER SEVENTEEN

Rachel bit her lower lip as she read the headline, "A new love match between Senator Robinson's Amish niece and a family friend." Below the false headline was a picture of Nick looking at her while they sat on the bench on the beach. "I didn't know Mr. Sullivan took this picture. I hope Samuel never sees this. We're sitting close together because the bench is small but you can't tell that from the picture. We were talking about our mothers. It wasn't anything romantic at all, even though it looks like it." She added that information for Violet's benefit. How could Mr. Sullivan do something so dishonest?

Her uncle had gone to the store and picked up a couple of popular Sunday newspapers. Adam, Violet, and Aunt Carrie were also relaxing on the deck with Rachel. They'd been enjoying the lovely weather and drinking lemonade. Violet had just teased Rachel about wearing flip flops again with her Plain dress and apron when her uncle returned from the store. She didn't mind Violet's teasing and loved feeling the sun on her bare feet.

"No wonder Sullivan didn't call you back," Aunt Carrie said to her husband.

"I stopped to see his aunt after I saw the pictures, and she said he left yesterday. Apparently, his ex-wife became ill and is in the hospital. The aunt didn't know he'd sold his pictures and apologized."

Violet leaned closer to Rachel to look at the pictures. She pointed to one with Rachel walking on the beach. "I bet he took that one our first day here. He lied when said he was taking pictures of the ocean and you happened to be in them. Obviously, he took them on purpose with you in the beach ones. He even managed to get one of us playing volleyball. Your smiling face at Nick supports you're having fun with him and could be a couple. I wonder how much money Mr. Sullivan got for these pictures."

"I'm sure he made a great deal of money from them." Adam cleared his throat. "Rachel, I'm sorry about the picture of you and Nick. Samuel's a pretty level-headed guy, but if you were my girlfriend and I saw this picture, I'd think there was something you weren't telling me."

Violet frowned. "Adam, they aren't kissing or—"

"But it's obviously taken on the beach and at night."

Rachel knew what Adam meant. A romance was implied in the heading, and the picture depicted an intimacy. And the cover-up she wore over her swimsuit didn't reach her knees. Why had she suggested they talk while sitting on the bench? Bare legs, sitting close to Nick, a lovely night on the beach...Samuel would have every right to question her about this picture. "You make a valid point, Adam. If he sees it, I'm sure I'll have some explaining to do. But Samuel probably won't see it unless someone tells him about it."

"Like Mary Zook," Violet said.

"Who's Mary Zook?" Aunt Carrie asked, leaning down to pick up a cookie from a plate in front of her. "I better grab the last cookie. Rachel, you make the best cookies."

"She's an Amish girl interested in Samuel." Violet squeezed Rachel's arm. "Not that she has a chance with him."

Aunt Carrie reached for the newspaper. "Let me see the pictures. I want to see if there's anything for your father to get upset about. I know David likes to read newspapers." She glanced at her husband. "That's one thing he has in common with you. But really, Rachel, you didn't pose for them. Sullivan was sneaky about it. Even though, he mentioned the beach shots, he didn't say he was selling the ones with you in them to the newspaper."

"I wonder if his Aunt Donna told the truth about him leaving the area." Uncle Scott finished his lemonade before putting it back on the table. "He must've decided the shots he had were good enough without getting ones of just our family. I get that it's probably because you're Amish, but still I wonder why he was so interested in you, Rachel."

"Dad, you're big news in the media. The press and many people in both parties predict that you'll run for president someday, so the fact Rachel's Amish makes it even more fascinating. Everyone's interested in how the

Amish can live so differently from us." Adam grinned at her. "Of course, after living with Violet for a few days, I bet you'll ready to return to Fields Corner."

She laughed. "You have something in common with Peter. He's a tease too. And I've enjoyed spending time with Violet."

Violet rolled her eyes at Adam. "You noticed that Rachel didn't mention you. Her visit went downhill after you arrived."

Holding the paper in her hands, Aunt Carrie said, "One nice thing in this article is the name of the beach isn't mentioned. It just says we're vacationing on a beach in Florida. Hopefully, we won't be bothered the rest of the time here by photographers and reporters."

"Since I'm leaving tomorrow morning, I hope you're right." Uncle Scott's looked at Aunt Carrie. "I might surprise everyone and leave politics."

"Don't do that, Dad. I want to work this summer with Nick."

"If I get out of politics, it'll be after I finish this term."

At the sound of Aunt Carrie's cell phone, she glanced at the caller ID. "I don't recognize the number and it says unknown caller. The area code is Fields Corner's. I better answer it. Maybe it's David returning your call."

Rachel hadn't gotten to talk to anyone last evening when she called Peter's phone. After she left a message, she'd been disappointed no one had called her back.

Her aunt's forehead creased as she said, "David, it's you. When I saw the number on my caller ID, I wondered who it could be. Is everything okay?"

How could my daed learn about the pictures so quickly? Maybe it was something else. Did he want her to come home early? It must be too much for Judith with teaching and going home to take care of the house.

"That's wonderful news," her aunt said. "I'm glad you put a phone in."

"What? My *daed* actually got a phone," she said in a surprised voice while Aunt Carrie continued her phone conversation. She figured he had called from Peter's.

"Well, that's good the boys are back home and safe now. I'll let you talk with Rachel. I don't want to run up your first phone bill too much." Aunt Carrie walked across the room, handing her the phone.

What had Matthew and Noah done now? She told them to behave while she was gone. Putting the phone next to her ear, she said, "Hello, *Daed.*"

"Hi, Rachel. Sorry I didn't know you called until today. Peter and Ella got home late last night. Peter and I built a shanty and the phone was just installed Friday afternoon."

Her *daed* spoke in such a rush which was unusual for him. He must be nervous using his new phone. Or was he uncomfortable talking to her? She needed to tell him soon how she didn't blame him any longer. In the past, she'd been curt whenever she said anything to him.

"It came in handy already. I was just telling Carrie how Matthew and Noah decided yesterday to get on a Greyhound bus to Florida. They wanted to see you and the dolphins." He chuckled. "I think you were the first priority in wanting to go to Florida, but the dolphins might have been a close second."

"I guess you used the phone to find them." She glanced at Aunt Carrie putting the empty glasses on a tray. Uncle Scott slid the door open for her as she carried them toward the kitchen.

"Instead of wasting time to see if they took off for Peter's, I called him and he called Samuel to see if he'd seen them. Fortunately, Mary Zook had seen them in town."

She was disappointed that her father hadn't called Samuel. She missed him and wondered how Samuel was doing. Maybe she should call Mary and ask her about Samuel. She seemed to be everywhere. Mary Zook's name kept cropping up a lot lately. "I'm glad they didn't get a ride and were safe."

"Wait a minute, Matthew. He's pestering me to give him the phone. Before I do, how are you?"

"I'm fine." *Should I mention the pictures?* Just as quickly that question occurred to her, she decided not to because she hadn't posed for them, and that could wait until later. "Did you get my postcard?"

"We got it yesterday afternoon. I promised the boys they could talk to you today, and Judith is here, too, so she wants to say hi after the boys' turn. Here's Matthew."

The next several minutes she talked to both Matthew and Noah. She loved hearing about their dolphin papers and their latest adventure into town. She cautioned both boys not to try again to get a ride to Florida, but she reassured them that they'd get a chance to visit the ocean too. And it might be soon.

When Judith got on the phone, she said, "I sent a letter out to you on Thursday after school. It has something important in it."

"I can't wait. What is it?" She hoped Judith decided to go to the Sunday singings. Her sister needed to get away from books once in a while and meet new people.

"It's about the whole phone thing. *Daed* told me that he wanted to put a phone in but *Mamm* didn't want it."

"Why in the world wouldn't she want a phone? She had to go to Maddox's house a lot to use their phone."

"I think she liked getting out of the house and visiting with Mrs. Maddox. They had a *wunderbaar* friendship and remember how *Mamm* loved babies. She seemed to especially like to visit Mrs. Maddox after she had her last baby."

"I guess I didn't realize how often she visited with Mrs. Maddox when she had a new baby."

"You were busy working at Weaver's Bakery and fall-ing in love with a certain furniture maker."

She giggled. "That's true. Back then, I had a job I loved, and I got to eat lunch daily with Samuel."

"One more thing is that *Daed* said that they were a team when it came to making family decisions, but when it came to household expenses and things, *Mamm* made the decisions. So she said no to a phone. It wasn't *Daed*."

"I don't understand why he never mentioned this to me."

"I don't know. He just told me. Maybe he thought we knew and he wished he'd gone ahead and put a phone in. He does feel terrible about not taking her to the doctor when she complained about not feeling well. Mrs. Maddox had offered to take her to the doctor, but she refused."

"I'm glad you told me about the phone situation and Mrs. Maddox's offer. I actually decided to forgive *Daed* a couple of days ago, but now I realize there wasn't anything to forgive him for." She took a deep breath. "How's it going with all the work you got stuck with?"

"I'm never going to be a great cook, but I think I've improved. It's working out okay except for the fact, the boys went missing yesterday. I was sewing new pants for them and lost track of time."

"I can't believe they tried to travel to see me. I'll be home soon. I miss all of you but I'm glad I got away. Hey, where are the boys and *Daed* now?" She noticed a few minutes ago, it was quiet in the background.

"They left to shoot basketballs. *Daed's* even playing with them."

She didn't remember her father ever playing basketball with Matthew and Noah. That was nice. After a couple more minutes of talking, they ended the call. Running up the phone bill for one call wouldn't be sensible. But it was *gut* to talk to her family.

This was a happy day, she thought, giving a broad smile to Violet and Adam. They didn't notice, though, because Violet was playing a game on her cell while Adam read the paper.

The morning started out pleasant with a walk on the beach with the whole Robinson family before they got dressed for church. She stayed home to read the Bible and to pray by herself. It worked out that she wasn't missing her district's church meeting, because today was the off-week. Everything had been great until Uncle Scott brought home the papers hinting at a romance between her and Nick. Unbelievable. Then her *daed* called and he didn't mention the pictures. It was nice to hear how her family missed her, too, but not that her brothers tried to travel to see her. The amazing news about a phone shanty on their property surprised her.

God had never stopped loving her, even when she was angry at her *daed.* He'd blessed her with many wonderful people. Especially Samuel. He'd surely understand if he heard about the picture of her with Nick. Wouldn't he? Or would he think she went on her rumspringe to enjoy a few dates with an Englisher... like her Aunt Carrie did at her age.

She would try not to worry and focus on what Jesus said in Matthew, "Don't be anxious about tomorrow. God will take care of your tomorrow too. Live one day at a time."

* * *

While walking on the beach with her husband, Carrie wondered about his earlier statement. *Was Scott serious about leaving politics?* She couldn't imagine him not being a politician. He was so good at it, but she did feel a moment of happiness that he was considering it. "Honey, were you kidding about not running again for senator?"

He gently squeezed her hand. "I like trying to make our country better, but I hate the corruptness that exists.

I never realized how flawed people could be and how far political people will go to get what they want."

"But you aren't like that. You've done a lot of good by being a senator. People love you."

"I'm afraid I'm not strong enough, and I'll become corrupt by the system too. That's why I'm afraid to stay in politics too long."

"You won't become corrupt. I won't let it happen. I'll be your moral conscience."

"Seeing the picture of Rachel and Nick in the paper also was a reminder of how the media twists everything. If I ever ran for president, I know reporters would camp out in front of our house and David's. Being connected to an Amish family would give them something else to write about. You know Rachel reminds me a lot of you at that age. Your Amish upbringing has made our family stronger." He stopped walking, pulling her to him. Bending his head, he kissed her and she returned it, savoring every moment of his lips on hers. His kiss was as tender and light as the ocean breeze. When the kiss ended, he murmured, "I love you, Carrie. I miss you when I'm away from home."

"I love you too. We need to pray about what you should do. God will guide us." She gazed at the waves hitting the shore. "It's beautiful tonight. I'm glad you could come here this weekend."

"It went too fast," he said as they resumed walking.

"I learned something about myself this past week with Rachel being here. Remember, how depressed I was when we went to Fields Corner to attend the funerals for my parents and Irene."

"It was overwhelming and very sad."

"Well, some of it was because I resented that I had left my Amish community. I missed not being around my parents, Irene and her family. I loved growing up Plain, and it never occurred to me that I wouldn't join the church. Life was simple and wonderful. After their deaths, I kept wondering if I had been living in Fields Corner if I would've realized Irene needed to see a doctor. I've examined my life a lot with Rachel asking me different questions."

"What did you learn?"

"That Irene might have still died. I can't blame myself and I made the right choice in marrying you." She gave him a playful nudge and said, "It's good you weren't a senator when we met. I don't think I could've married a politician. But seriously, I know blending our backgrounds was the best for Adam and Violet. We each brought wonderful qualities to our marriage. We both simplify our lives whenever things get too insane and hectic. I think we realize more than some couples how important it is to mesh our ideas and stick to our basic priorities in life. "

He grinned. "Whew, that's a relief. As much as I admire the Amish faith, I don't think I could go without electricity and drive a buggy."

"I don't think you could either."

"Maybe you should be the politician. You've been the force behind me working hard for all the promises I made during my campaigns."

"Me running for an office will never happen." She teased, "But if you decide not to run again, I could enjoy not making speeches. And I'm sure your constituents will be thankful for that too."

"How about we go back to the deck and smooch? The kids are probably in bed by now."

"Especially Rachel. She gets up early to walk on the beach. Violet's even walked with her a couple of times during the early morning hours. I'm glad the girls enjoyed spending time together. Violet has introduced Rachel to new things to experience that she won't be able to do once she joins the church. In turn, Rachel has explained the Amish way of life to Violet. She asked Rachel tons of questions. Violet also seems to like learning Pennsylvania Dutch. I should've taught it to Adam and Violet before." She paused for a moment. "Maybe Violet will decide to become Amish."

She heard his quick intake of breath before he spoke. "That surprised me for a second until I realized you were kidding. Our daughter is the Queen of Twitter and has a Facebook obsession." He laughed. "Can you imagine her withdrawal from our world? She gets upset if we're somewhere for a short time with no cell phone reception."

"That's true. She hates when a snowstorm knocks out the power too."

"We should rinse the sand off our feet before going in." She stopped by the faucet at the foot of the steps, turning it on and carefully rinsing off each foot before putting her flip flops back on.

While Scott rinsed off the sand, she said, "Rachel seemed pretty happy to talk with David. I know she's forgiven him. She told me so the other day."

After they climbed the steps and were seated next to each other on the deck, Scott put his arm around her. "We should invite Rachel and her family to go to Outer Banks with us this summer. They can get a ride to our house. We can rent a big van."

"That's a good idea. It'll have to be when David's not as busy in the fields. Maybe Peter and Ella could come at a time that Adam's at our beach house. That way there will always be one of them home to take care of their livestock."

"You're one clever woman. Always thinking of everything."

"Now, how about the smooching you promised me. Don't you dare renege on this promise, Senator Robinson."

"I wouldn't think of it. It's one promise I mean to keep."

She quivered at the sweet tenderness of his kiss.

CHAPTER EIGHTEEN

Early Monday morning, Rachel gazed at the vastness of the ocean. She wore the tan capris and blue blouse she bought on the shopping trip with Violet. Since Mr. Sullivan and Nick had left Cocoa Beach, she'd decided not to wear her Plain clothing in the morning. The only people she saw on the beach weren't close. It would probably be the last time she wore her English clothing. She'd give the few purchased pieces of clothing to Violet, except for the swimming suit. That she'd be able to wear again. Briefly she touched her ponytail, thinking how she didn't pin her hair up this morning.

The gentle waves smacking against her feet soothed her spirit while she sat on a low beach chair. For a few minutes, she watched a few dolphins in the distance jumping out of the crystal blue water. *I wish the twins could see them with me.*

Peace washed over her as she continued praying, giving thanks for all her blessings. She thought how even Jesus had gone to lonely places to pray. Yesterday during her Bible reading, she recalled it said in one of the chapters in Luke, *"But he withdrew himself in the deserts, and prayed."* God had meant for her to visit the ocean. He knew she needed to get away from family and focus on what had turned her world upside down when *Mamm* died suddenly. Here, she'd fully opened up to her heavenly Father. She hadn't been able to do this at home.

After giving her bitterness and problems to God during this week and forgiving her father in her heart, she'd realized her *mamm* missed them. But *Mamm* was happy to be in heaven. *Mamm* would be glad she no longer blamed *Daed.* That was a certainty. Even if there had been a phone nearby to use, *Mamm* could've died. Going to an English doctor might have made a difference, and she would still be alive. Why didn't she ask Mrs. Maddox to give her a ride? Whenever one of her children needed to see a doctor, *Mamm* hadn't hesitated to get a ride for them.

Tears racked her body. Moisture pooled in her eyes, blurring the vision of the ocean. She missed her *mamm* so much. Maybe someday Fields Corner would have a medical facility with all kinds of physicians. But obviously, it had been Irene Hershberger's time to die a year ago as written in Ecclesiastes, "To everything there is a season, and a time to every purpose in heaven. A time to be born and a time to die; a time to plant, and a time to reap that which is planted."

She took a deep breath of the air while finishing her thoughts and prayers. After she stood, she folded the chair. Around nine o'clock she'd call Samuel at the furniture store. She couldn't wait to talk to him and tell him how she'd decided to join the church. Tomorrow they were starting back to Kentucky. Violet needed to take a flight out of Kentucky on Wednesday afternoon. Her college classes started again on Thursday. Adam was going to help drive and stay at home for a couple of days before flying back to his college.

* * *

"Aunt Carrie, you look pretty." Rachel said. Her aunt was going to drive Uncle Scott to the airport. She wore a pale pink sundress with a light white sweater. She'd gotten a shade darker from enjoying the seashore so her bare legs looked great in white, strappy and elegant sandals.

"*Danki.*" Aunt Carrie held her phone out to her. "Here's my phone. Samuel will be happy to hear your voice."

Glancing at the kitchen clock, she saw it was nine o'clock. "I can't wait any longer. He sometimes enjoys a cup of coffee in the bakery before going to his store but I'll try to get him now."

Aunt Carrie grinned. "I'm sure he only did that when you were working at Weaver's Bakery. I doubt he's sitting in the bakery without his favorite girl around."

The phone rang once. Her jaw dropped when she heard a female voice saying, "Hello. Weaver's Furniture Store."

"Hello. Is Samuel there?"

"Rachel, is that you? I'm Samuel's secretary right now. First, I got a job at the bakery. I suppose even in Florida, you heard that bit of news. Mrs. Weaver really needed the help. Now I get to answer the phone for Samuel."

She clenched her jaw. *Mary Zook is now answering Samuel's business phone. Why did Samuel need to hire Mary Zook, of all people? And why did he even need a secretary?* "Mary, I'd—"

"Guess what?"

Does she ever shut up, Rachel wondered as Mary didn't give her a chance to ask to speak to Samuel. She better listen to Mary's chatter.

"And he loved it. He enjoyed me bringing him a slice of the coffeecake with a nice cup of steaming coffee. You really should try this recipe for Samuel if you return to Fields Corner. Oh, here's Samuel now."

"Hi, Rachel. I'm glad you called."

"Is Mary really your secretary now?"

"No, she's not. Hold on for a second. Mary's going back to the bakery. I want to thank her for the coffeecake she brought this morning."

When Samuel returned, he said, "I was in the back looking over some new wood when Mary answered the phone. She came back over to see if I wanted another piece of coffeecake." He chuckled. "Don't worry. It wasn't as good as yours."

"I guess Mary's trying to impress you with all her baking skills while I'm away. It's definitely a small world. While Violet and I walked on the beach the other day, we met a cousin of Mary's. Apparently, Mary told them she likes working at the bakery because it's next to your furniture store and she's interested in you."

He sighed. "I've been trying to avoid her as much as possible. She even tried to get me to take her home after work, but I've avoided that so far."

"I got your letter. It was *wunderbaar* receiving it. I have so much to tell you. After praying I realized how wrong I've been about a lot of things. I forgive my father and I shouldn't have blamed him. I made a big decision that will make you happy. I want to join the church. I'll talk to the bishop as soon as I get back to Fields Corner."

"I'm glad to hear that. I hope you can be baptized with Katie and Judith. How soon will you be home?"

"We're leaving here tomorrow morning for Kentucky. Violet needs to catch a flight back to college on Wednesday. Adam's going to help drive because Nick left yesterday to spend time with his father. I suppose Aunt Carrie will drive me home as soon as Adam goes back to college."

"I wish I could get a driver to take me to Kentucky on Wednesday and get you, but that won't be possible."

She heard the door chime in the background. She hoped it wasn't Mary again. "Do you have a customer? I heard the door opening."

"*Ya.* Actually two came into the store. I'll let them look around for a few minutes."

She decided to mention the pictures of her and Nick. Although Samuel might never learn about the one photo and headline implying a romantic time on the bench, she would feel better explaining what happened. "Samuel, I want to tell you something. That photographer, Mr. Sullivan, sold pictures of me on the beach. Also one of our volleyball games was in the newspaper. I didn't pose for any of the pictures. He even sold one of me talking with Nick about our mothers dying. He made it look like we were intimate and it wasn't like that at all."

"How did Sullivan manage to do that?"

"Nick asked me to walk with him on the beach to talk. I'd been swimming in the pool while everyone was inside the house. I wasn't expecting him to come out to the pool but I went for a short walk with him. We sat on a bench but it was small. We were not sitting close because of a romantic thing at all. Unfortunately, Mr. Sullivan made it seem like we wanted to be close to each other. You can't tell from the photo, that the bench is small. I'm afraid the headlines imply we are romantically involved, which is not true at all. I love you, Samuel."

"I love you too. I'm glad you told me about it. I wouldn't be surprised if it wasn't all innocent on Nick's part."

She exhaled a deep breath. "He seemed a bit interested in me, but I never gave him any encouragement. I'm hoping he'll realize how great Violet is. She's crazy about him."

"Rachel, you're a beautiful woman. It bothers me a little that Nick saw you in your swimsuit, but I trust and believe you that nothing happened."

"As soon as I got out of the pool, I put Aunt Carrie's cover-up on." She didn't add that Nick helped her with the cover-up. That piece of information wouldn't go over big with Samuel. "If I'd known he was coming out to the pool, I wouldn't have gone swimming. I thought he was going to watch a movie with the others." Now that she got the whole newspaper picture thing out of the way, she didn't want to talk about Nick any longer. "Do you need to check on your customers?"

"They're still browsing. I'll check on them soon. First, I need to tell you something. I planned on calling you today to tell you that my *mamm's* youngest sister died suddenly. We're going to Kenton tomorrow to be there for her funeral. Peter's going to take care of our livestock. Mary and a couple of her friends are going to take care of the bakery customers. I'll close my store for Tuesday and Wednesday."

"Tell your mother I'm sorry about her sister. That's going to be hard on the ten children and husband she leaves behind."

"I know. *Mamm* never thought her baby sister would go first. But God knows best. It's just hard on us when someone close and dear to us leaves this world. Apparently my aunt complained of a backache and stomach ache after the birth of her youngest baby. She went to the doctor but it was too late. She died of a ruptured appendix."

"That's so sad. At first she must have thought the pain came from childbirth."

"My uncle told the children how she'd gone to sleep and that she's now in heaven with God. I think he's still in shock that she's gone but he's trying to cope as well as he can." He cleared his throat. "We should be back late on Wednesday. If you aren't here, I can see if I can get a driver to take me to your Aunt Carrie's."

"I can't wait to see you. I've miss you and my family." She should mention to Samuel that she wanted to return to work in the bakery. Hopefully, not on the days Mary's there. *Or maybe it'd be better to work when the eager Mary is there, so I can keep track of her. That's silly. I don't need to worry about Samuel becoming interested in Mary.* "You might say something to your *mamm* that I want to start working at the bakery a couple days of the week. Of course, she might not need me now with Mary working for her."

"Are you kidding? *Mamm* will be thrilled to have you back. Me too. We can eat our lunch together again. I'm definitely happy you went to the ocean now. Getting away from Fields Corner seemed to work miracles. Hey, your twin brothers wanted to get away too. Did you hear how they wanted to get on a bus and travel all the way to Florida just to see you?"

"Yes, *Daed* called me from his new phone, and I heard about it. I'm glad he got the phone."

"One of the customers is looking at me. I better go. I'll see you soon. Bye, Rachel."

After she said a hurried bye to Samuel, she looked for Aunt Carrie. She found her knitting a prayer shawl by a huge window in the living room. "Here's your phone. I thought you had to go soon to the airport."

Aunt Carrie stopped knitting to look at her. "Scott's making several business calls before we leave. How's Samuel?"

She repeated what Samuel told her about going to his aunt's funeral with the rest of his family. Then concluded with, "Samuel said he can get a driver and get me at your house. That way you won't have to make another long trip to drive me home."

"That's sweet of Samuel. I have a feeling he's anxious to see you. I can drive you home Wednesday after we drop Violet off at the airport. I'll just spend the night and enjoy time with my other niece and nephews." Aunt Carrie laughed. "I wonder what it'd be like if my whole family lived at home. That's definitely a strong advantage to being Amish. Families aren't living apart and running off all the time to other places. With our cars and planes, we make it easy for our children to leave us. My house will be empty again."

"I'm sorry," she said, sitting on a small couch.

"I miss being a teacher's assistant but I'm considering going to college." Her blue eyes widened. "Can you imagine me going to college at my age?"

"That's a wonderful idea. What are you going to study?"

"I enjoyed helping the children with their reading and felt I was good at it, so I'd like to become a reading specialist." She put the shawl in a tote bag. "I have some-thing I want you to have." Aunt Carrie walked through the open doorway to the kitchen.

I wonder what she wants me to have. When she watched Aunt Carrie pick her purse off the table, she hoped it wasn't money.

While Aunt Carrie zipped open an inside pouch, she said, "I know, of course, that Amish don't have pictures of loved ones, but I think you should have one of your mother. I didn't want it to get bent so it's in a paper frame inside this envelope."

After the envelope was in her hands, Rachel slid out the picture. Her eyes filled with tears while she gazed at her mother's lovely face. She looked carefree and happy sitting at their picnic table. "It's a *wunderbaar* picture of *Mamm*. Did you take it?"

"Yes. I snapped it of her during the last visit I made be-fore our parents were killed. I showed it to Irene on my digital camera. She laughed and said that I was always the sneaky one in the family. She hadn't been aware of me taking her picture." Aunt Carrie paused for a moment. "Irene had a great laugh. The kind of belly laugh that was contagious and made other people feel good inside."

"She did have an awesome laugh. We used to laugh a lot together. She had a *wunderbaar* sense of humor."

With a tissue from her purse, Aunt Carrie wiped her eyes. She sniffed a few times, then said, "I took the pic-ture on the day you and the others played croquet in the front yard. I know how hard all of this has been on you, losing your sweet mother. It seems unfair her life was cut short already, but I remind myself that we must not question God's will. He works in mysterious ways. We need to remember all the good times we had with her. Irene was a strong and beautiful woman with a compassionate heart. She had such a joyful interest in each person she met and as you know, was hard-working. She was a great helpmate for your father."

"*Danki* for this picture. I'll always treasure it."

"People have asked me how Amish women can live such an oppressed lifestyle. I tell them how wrong that perception is, and how Amish women base their lives on Christian understanding and practices. The Plain lifestyle works so well because of the committed women making it continue for all of them."

"That's an advantage with you being raised Amish but now living as an English woman. You can explain our Plain way of life so well to others." She remembered what Judith had told her yesterday during their phone conversation about their parents' relationship. "Amish women are definitely in charge of many things in their lives, and we are not burdened. *Daed* and *Mamm* made many decisions together."

"Those two had a great marriage. The past year has been rough on your father."

"Do you think I can follow in *Mamm's* footsteps and be a good wife and mother?" Her mother had done so much for all of them, and never complained about anything.

Aunt Carrie put an arm around her shoulders. "I have no doubt that you'll be a *wunderbaar* wife and mother. Just like Irene was to you and the others."

"I'd like to show this picture to Judith but not to Matthew and Noah." She grinned. "They can't keep their mouths shut. I don't need to get in trouble before I even get a chance to talk to our bishop about joining the church."

"I can give a picture to Judith, but I agree we'll wait a few years to mention pictures of your mother to the boys."

* * *

Late Monday afternoon, Rachel sat on her bed to read Judith's letter. Although her sister had told her a few things on the phone yesterday that were probably in the letter, she looked forward to reading Judith's thoughts.

Dear Rachel,

Samuel said that he talked to you and you arrived safely. I hope you are enjoying the beach. We are study-ing dolphins in school and the twins are wondering if you've seen any. Both boys did an excellent job on their reports about dolphins. Matthew made a clay model of a dolphin to include with his paper.

I have something important to tell you. I even thought of calling you from our school phone, but de-cided to write instead. I had a conversation with Daed the other night. I learned that he wanted to put a phone in a few years ago but mamm didn't want him to. She said it was an extra expense and wasn't needed. Remember how mamm enjoyed going to visit with Mrs. Maddox when she needed to make doctor appointments. I think using the neighbors' phone gave her an excuse to take a break and enjoy another woman's company during the day.

So, Rachel, it wasn't Daed not wanting the phone but Mamm. He said when it came to household matters; he let mamm make the decisions. Other matters, they many times made decisions together. He said how they had been a team.

I was angry at first at mamm that she didn't take Mrs. Maddox's offer to drive her to see the doctor, but I'm not now. My anger wasn't going to bring her back to us.

Daed's unhappy that Bishop Amos wants him to consider remarrying. The Bishop even has someone picked out for our daed. His sister. Apparently, she's going to visit Bishop Amos soon. Daed's not interested. He misses mamm so much.

Today I read in Romans a verse that made me think how we must remember that God's will is best. We can't judge others based on what we think is right or what we think is the cause behind any sadness. Society judges but we must forgive like Jesus did on the cross.

Be careful in the ocean water. If you see anything that remotely looks like a shark, get out of the water. I read that sharks migrate when spring is on the way. The two species that migrate up the east coast from the Caribbean are spinners and blacktip. They don't eat people *but like to bite. They might think your hand or foot is a fish. From what I read, they are responsible for a third of Florida's shark bites. Once they realize they aren't biting a fish, they let go. Hopefully, the shark migration is over in Florida, but in case it isn't, I thought I should pass this on. I'd hate for you to get bitten by a shark.*

Give Aenti Carrie and Violet my love.

Your loving sister in Christ,

Judith

P.S. We all miss you. I haven't burned down the house yet. And no one has lost weight from my cooking.

Even though, she had already forgiven her father, she was glad Judith's letter arrived before leaving Cocoa Beach. The Bible verse Judith referred to in her letter about not conforming to the pattern of this world made her feel strongly she was making the right decisions about her life. Nothing could stop her from telling the bishop she wanted to be baptized and to join their church. Part of her doubts had come from her mother dying young, but Nick's mother died in a car accident. Life was fragile whether you were Amish or English.

She took clothes out of the oak dresser to pack. Before folding them, she glanced at her surroundings. Falling asleep in a queen size bed to the sound of ocean waves had been heavenly. She'd miss seeing the beautiful sunrise over the ocean water.

Taking a break from her daily routine of working hard daily for her siblings and father had been crucial in facing what was lacking in her character. She'd worked through her negative feelings and been freed from her bitterness about her mother's death.

She would never regret going on her *rumspringe* and experiencing firsthand the English way of life. Spending time on the beach with her relatives had been eye-opening. Watching how Violet liked to tweet about everything was fun, but it was not for her. She heard the little ping from Violet's cell phone constantly, signaling each time she received a text message. Really, it seemed a waste of time to her. She'd done various English pastimes: experimented with a bit of makeup, wore English clothes, watched movies and television, used Violet's laptop, and drove a car. It'd been wonderful and exciting to try each new item on Violet's list. But none of these things were going to influence her enough to leave her Amish faith.

It surprised her to read about Bishop Amos telling their *daed* to consider getting married a second time. Was it because she had left Fields Corner to figure out if she wanted to be Amish? Or had the bishop thought she wasn't doing a good job taking care of her family? No one could replace *Mamm*. She had tried but it was impossible. She didn't regret giving up her full-time job at the bakery to try to do her best at taking over doing all the domestic work, but it was time to delegate a few of the household duties to Judith. She'd be done with teaching the end of May, so maybe during the summer months; she could even work more than two days a week at the bakery.

Violet entered the bedroom, wearing brown shorts with an orange T-shirt. She gave her an unhappy look.

"You should roll your clothes instead of folding them. They'll be less wrinkled when you unpack."

"Thanks. I'll do that. What's wrong? Are you unhappy about leaving the beach?"

Violet started rolling one of her aprons. "Nick wants to see you again. I heard Adam on the phone give Nick your address."

"Why would Adam do that? He knows I love Samuel."

"Adam reminded Nick that you're serious about Samuel." Violet sighed. "Not only is Nick smoking hot, but he's a good guy. I knew he'd end up falling in love with you but was hoping I'd be wrong."

"He hasn't fallen in love with me... you're exaggerating. It's just a passing infatuation on Nick's part. I'm from a different world and that must be exciting to him, for some reason. Also he must feel a connection because we both lost our mothers." She dropped her rolled dress in the bag. "I made it clear to Nick that I like being Amish. He asked me if I met the right non-Amish guy, if I would marry him. I told him that I love Samuel. You'll be working with him this summer and he'll see what a wonderful person you are. You're funny, pretty and smart."

Violet frowned. "There's more. Nick tweeted he met the most wonderful girl who he wants to marry." Placing the apron in her luggage, Violet continued, "When is your wedding to Samuel? Soon, I hope. When you're out of the picture, maybe Nick will notice me, because he'll have to forget about you becoming Mrs. Foster."

"It depends when I get baptized. I have to become a church member before Samuel and I get married. Samuel already joined the church so we might get married in November." She didn't add it might be later because Violet's brown eyes looked so sad.

Samuel had said in his letter they could wait until she was ready. Was she ready to get married in less than a year? She would be twenty-one next month.

CHAPTER NINETEEN

Samuel couldn't wait to get the milking done. When they arrived home from their trip to Kenton, he had right away checked their answering machine in the barn. He'd been happy to hear that Rachel was already home. He left a message on Aunt Carrie's phone, saying he'd come over as soon as he finished milking their cows. Well, not right away. He didn't want to smell like the barn, so he'd take a shower and put fresh clothes on.

While milking he thought how their English driver had asked if they milked their cows by hand. Their usual driver couldn't take them to Kenton, but said his cousin would be able to make the trip. She had asked his family tons of question about the Amish life. She'd been surprised to learn that very few Amish milked their cows by hand. His *daed* explained to the young English woman that they used modern milking equipment and had modern refrigerated milk tanks.

"But I thought you didn't use electricity," she said while driving them in her parents' minivan.

"We use gas-powered equipment for our barn and for our water heaters, stoves and refrigerators. Gas-pressured lanterns and lamps are used to light our homes, shops, and other buildings."

Milking wasn't his favorite thing so Samuel was thankful to have a growing customer list for his furniture business. Having his own small farm would be perfect for him and his future family needs.

"Jacob and I'll finish up here," his *daed* said. "You go see Rachel."

"*Danki, Daed.*"

* * *

Rachel smoothed her dark green dress before putting a clean apron over it. Judith had a chicken casserole in the oven for their supper, while she'd made a butterscotch pie for Samuel and peanut butter cookies for the boys. From her bedroom, she could hear both Matthew and Noah yell, "Whoopee."

It was great to be home, she thought, and to listen to her brothers' happy voices. She hadn't been gone for long but just the short time away made her look at her home life differently. Before she hurried out of her bedroom to see what the boys were excited about, she took *Mamm's* picture out of her bureau's drawer. She prayed, "Dear Lord, my gracious God, *danki* for my sweet *mamm* and my *wunderbaar* family."

As she entered the kitchen, fragrant smells of baking bread filled the room. Aunt Carrie had gone to work instantly when they arrived home and made several loaves of bread.

Judith gave her a broad smile. "I see how it is. You made a butterscotch pie for Samuel and you have a green dress on. Doesn't Samuel like both? I guess I better take lessons from my sister on how to please a man."

"*Schweschder*, you need to get a boyfriend first. You aren't staying home anymore when I go to Sunday singings. You'll be eighteen in May. It'll be a great time to start attending them." The past year she hadn't made enough of an effort to include Judith when she'd socialize with other young people. She'd invited her a few times and had given up when Judith expressed no interest in going. When it came to teaching a roomful of students, Judith wasn't shy, but around young men, she was. She'd been surprised that no young man had been persistent in getting Judith's attention. Her sister looked pretty in her deep purple dress. Her cheeks were rosy, probably from checking on the casserole in the oven.

"I'm worried about getting my GED. I'll go to the Sunday singings after I pass my test. I should have already taken it."

She knew it was important to Judith to receive the equivalent of a high school diploma. She loved being a teacher so had continued her studies after eight grade via correspondence schools. By educating herself, their parents had been happy to see their daughter keeping the Amish philosophy of staying apart from the world. Even so, they had worried at times that Judith might want to continue her education at college and not join the church. "I'm sure you will pass the first GED examination with one of the highest scores ever received in Ohio."

She turned from Judith to look at her two brothers, eating their cookies. "Don't fill up on cookies. Save some room for Judith's casserole. I can't believe I gave you permission to eat cookies so close to supper."

"I know why. You missed us a lot. You make the best cookies, Rachel." Noah took another bite of cookie

"*Aenti* Carrie said we can go to Outer Banks this summer." Matthew smiled at his aunt. She was seated between the boys at the long oak table at one end of the big kitchen.

Noah's green eyes widened, "She already asked *Daed* and he said yes."

Judith laughed. "I think he has several summer weekend trips planned so he'll be too busy to spend time with Bishop Amos' sister, Barbara."

Matthew leaned forward in his chair. "Will we take the bus to Outer Banks?"

Aunt Carrie shook her head. "No, we're thinking of coming here to get you and drive you to Outer Banks. We haven't worked out the details yet."

"Would you like another cup of coffee?" Rachel glanced at her aunt's empty coffee cup.

"Yes, please."

After refilling her aunt's cup, she glanced out of the window and saw Samuel hop out of his buggy. "Samuel's here." In one hurried motion, she grabbed her cape from the hook by the door and went outside. Samuel wouldn't be able to show her any affection in front of her family. It was not the Amish way for a dating couple to kiss in front of others. No kissing was to occur while courting, but they had kissed in private and held hands frequently. But that was all. They respected each other and wanted to remain pure in God's eyes before marriage.

"Hi, Samuel." She put her cape on while he hitched the horse to their post. Samuel's dark hair that barely touched his white shirt collar looked damp. He must've showered before coming to see her. When his gaze met hers, warmth spread through her body. Samuel must have felt the same way because his blue eyes brightened with pleasure.

"I'm glad you came out here." He drew Rachel to him and his lips came down on hers.

She melted into his strong, muscled arms. Their mouths met for a long, sweet kiss. The joyous way Samuel's lips covered hers revealed his own excitement at being together. When it ended, she looked up into his eyes and said, "Everything that concerned me before I left doesn't now. I want to talk to you more about it after supper."

"That's *gut*." He grinned. "Does that mean you might like to become Mrs. Samuel Weaver sometime?"

"Definitely." Out of the corner of her eye, she saw her father closing the door to the barn.

"How about we go for a buggy ride to my land later and talk more?"

"I like how you think. Before we go, you'll want to eat a piece of my butterscotch pie I made for you."

"You just got home and you made my favorite pie."

"You rate more than I do, Samuel. Rachel didn't make my favorite cookies, but I'm sure she will soon. She's a *gut* daughter." Her *daed* winked at both of them. "She'll make a fine wife."

"I didn't have any chocolate chips. I'll get them tomorrow and make you a big batch of cookies, *Daed*."

"Hey, it's time to eat. Get in here," Aunt Carrie called from the open door.

Her *daed* walked ahead of them to the house. "I timed that right. I just got done milking the cows."

* * *

Although the March day had been sunny and gone up to sixty degrees, the night air was extremely chilly. While they talked in Samuel's buggy on his land, she appreciated the blanket and hot chocolate in a thermos. She'd been surprised he still hadn't seen the picture of her with Nick on the bench. But maybe that was for the best.

Samuel was a good listener while she explained how she'd been wrong to blame her *daed* for her *mamm's* death. She mentioned how Nick's mother died in her forties from a car accident. Tragic things happened to English and to Amish.

"It was a shock that my Aunt Susan died suddenly. No one expected the youngest one to go first. *Mamm* and her brothers all thought the world of their baby sister."

"How old was she?"

"Thirty-seven. I'm glad we made the trip. *Mamm's* grief was made lighter by sharing it with other members of the community there. Her sister was loved by everyone. The *kinner* will have a hard time in the days ahead, but we saw many people already trying to ease the grief for them and giving them lots of attention. "

They didn't stay long because she hadn't gotten to talk to her *daed* a lot and wanted to before he went to bed. On the way back to Hershberger's farm, Rachel gazed at the sky. "The night is clear with lots of stars."

"So do you think you can live in boring Fields Corner instead of Cocoa Beach?"

She laughed. "You know I can. I loved the ocean but it's good to be home. I have so much to look forward to... working in your *mamm's* bakery again will be *gut.* Judith feels more comfortable now about balancing her teaching job with helping a bit more at home so I can work at the bakery." Samuel had said his *mamm* was *froh* she wanted to work a couple of days.

"I almost forgot. Katie wants to talk to you tomorrow. She told me to be sure to tell you. Apparently she has something big to discuss with you, but I have no clue what it is."

"I wonder what's on her mind." Was it something more about Tim? He must not be the right man for Katie. God must have someone else for her friend to marry. Or maybe she'd never marry. Not all Amish women married. She felt sorry for Katie. *I know her love for Tim is deep and it hurts her greatly that he's seeing an English woman.*

"Are you going to see the bishop soon?"

"*Ya.* I want to see him tomorrow."

"I still think we should go to the beach after we marry."

Not this again, she thought. "Samuel, you know better. Amish newlyweds don't go on a honeymoon. We'll spend our weekends throughout the winter visiting our family and other people. That's when they give us our wedding gifts. Don't you want to receive our gifts?"

"I meant we'd go later to the beach," he said as they stopped in front of her house.

"I'd love to go with you sometime."

He grinned. "How about a quick kiss before you go in?"

"It better be quick. I don't want anyone seeing us kiss." She chuckled. "You know how nosy my brothers are."

His lips brushed hers before she quickly left the buggy. She turned at the door to wave good-bye to Samuel. She realized it wasn't the length of the kiss that was important, but the sweet feeling she felt in her heart from his love.

She saw a light on in the living room and found her *daed* reading *The Budget.* "Does Judith have an article in this issue?"

He shook his head and neatly folded the paper. "No, she doesn't. Did you enjoy your buggy ride?"

"I did." She had to ask him why he never mentioned anything about *Mamm* being the one to say no to a phone. Crossing the polished wood floor, Rachel settled herself on a plain brown upholstered couch near to her *daed's* chair. "Why didn't you tell me that it was *Mamm* who didn't want a phone? I thought all the time that it was you that didn't want us to have a phone in the barn or to have a phone shanty. I learned this recently from Judith that it was *Mamm* who objected."

He shrugged. "It was too painful to talk about it to you. I should have tried harder to convince your mother that we needed a phone for emergencies. Or I could've taken a key for Maddox's house when they went on vacation so we could get inside to use their phone. Frank wanted to give me a house key. I thought just putting their mail in the breezeway was fine. The main regret I have is not taking your mother to a doctor. He probably would've suggested surgery to correct her heart problem. She would still be here with us if I'd been a better husband."

"We don't know that, *Daed*. It might not have made any difference. And if she had surgery, she could've died on the operating table. It wasn't your fault she died."

"I wish I could believe that."

"I'm sorry I haven't been nice to you. While I was away, I realized how wrong I was to blame you for *Mamm's* death. She could have arranged to have Mrs. Maddox or someone else drive her to the doctor. I guess we all thought she was tired because of not sleeping well with Grandma and Grandpa Troyer's deaths. She didn't say too much about her symptoms. It was easy to blame you, but I'm sorry. I went for early morning walks on the beach when it was quiet and peaceful and I prayed. I forgave you but later I realized I didn't need to forgive you for anything."

He squeezed her hand. "After the boys tried to run away, I did a lot of thinking too. I came to the conclusion that I depended on you too much. I should have told you to continue working at the bakery part-time. It's no wonder you resented me when I left a lot on your shoulders and Judith's too. I need to spend more time with Matthew and Noah. We never went boating last summer so want to do that as soon as the weather's warm enough."

"Do you think you'll have time?" She grinned. "I heard Bishop Amos wants you to court his sister."

He smiled back. "I might run away when she comes to Ohio." His expression became serious. "No one can take your *mamm's* place. I'm not interested in remarrying. Maybe in time I will but it's doubtful. I miss her all the time but it was God's will to take her. I'm thankful I still have my *kinner*. You look a lot like your *mamm* did at your age."

"I hope I'll be a good wife and mother someday like she was."

"You seem happier. Getting away for a week must have agreed with you. Did you get to experience enough of the English world? You weren't gone long."

She nodded. "I watched movies and television with Violet. Before we left Kentucky, I drove Violet's car on the side streets in their subdivision. I wore English clothes a few times while we were at the beach, but I felt weird not wearing my Plain clothing." She thought for a minute, trying to remember what else she did. "I think that's it except I did get on Violet's laptop a few times."

"Sounds like you did a lot in a short time." He leaned forward in his chair. "I'm glad you're home. The house wasn't the same without you."

"I missed you and everyone too." She felt relief apologizing to her *daed* for her past behavior. She noticed a few more wrinkles on his face and his hair looked grayer. This past year had been rough on the whole family. *I should tell Daed about my decision to become baptized.* "I'm going to talk to Bishop Amos tomorrow about taking instructions to join the church."

"That's *wunderbaar,* Rachel."

"I like how Amish parents allow their children to make their own decisions when to get baptized and whether to accept the Plain life. You and *Mamm* taught us well why you chose the Amish life but didn't shelter us from the non-Amish world. You took us out of our community to Wal-Mart and other English stores. We were exposed to all kinds of things in the outside world, but because of you and *Mamm's* solid convictions in being Amish, I'm ready to make a commitment to join the church."

"Your decision makes me *froh.* The most important thing is that I can tell it makes you happy too."

"I know why I love Samuel. He reminds me of you, *Daed.*"

Aunt Carrie stood in the doorway. "I'm sorry to interrupt, but Matthew and Noah are waiting for you. I told them about growing up with Irene and what kind of games we played. They want to see you before they fall asleep. They certainly love their big sister."

"*Danki.* I better go. I promised to tuck them in tonight."

While climbing the stairs to the boys' room, she thought how in less than a year, Samuel might be living in their house as her husband. Of course, they could finish their new house in time for them to move to right after their wedding, but she liked Samuel's suggestion to stay with her *daed* and her siblings at first. It'd be easier to help take care of her brothers if she wasn't in a separate house. Even if *Daed* changed his mind about remarrying, it wasn't going to happen soon. He definitely wasn't interested in anyone yet. Her family still needed her around.

"Hey, boys." She saw them both propped up in their bed with shiny clean faces.

"*Danki*, for our dolphin books and seashells." Matthew said.

"I'm glad you like my gifts." Matthew and Noah each had a book opened that she bought for them in Florida. She sat on the edge of the bed. "So did Aunt Carrie show you the pictures we took of the dolphins?"

Noah nodded. "They're great pictures. Could you hear the dolphins make any noises?"

"When they came above the water, I heard a few squeaking noises."

"I hope we hear them when we go to Outer Banks."

Matthew added, "I hope we actually see them too. You're lucky, Rachel. I can't wait until we go to the beach. I want to pick up seashells like you did."

"Well, just think I didn't go to the beach until I was almost twenty-one years old. If it works out and you go this summer, you'll only be eleven." She smiled. "You two are lucky. The beach is enjoyable but I'm happy to be home."

Noah, looking concerned, said, "I wonder if *Mamm* ever got to go to the ocean when she was our age."

"I don't think so because she never said anything about going to the seashore to me." Rachel thought for a moment. "And I'm sure she never went as an adult. Aunt Carrie and Uncle Scott bought their beach house in North Carolina around three or four years ago. If Aunt Carrie asked her to the beach, *Mamm* must have said no. *Mamm* never mentioned wanting to see the ocean. But she seemed the happiest when she was here at home."

Matthew grinned. "She liked to go to Target and Wal-Mart. She bought us candy bars sometimes."

"Maybe we can go in July and be at the ocean on our birthday." Noah closed his book. "Rachel, do you think that's possible?"

"*Ya*, I like that idea but it depends when it's a good time for *Daed* and Aunt Carrie and Uncle Scott. Don't forget *Daed* wants to go boating too. I suggest you two do your chores and listen to *Daed* and behave in school. You don't want to miss out on any of the fun this summer."

She hoped *Daed* would be able to go boating and relax some on Sundays. He worked hard as a farmer. He got up early to feed the animals, milk the cows and process the milk for delivery to the local dairy. Then he joined them for prayer and breakfast. Depending on the season, her *daed* worked in the fields, got the fields ready for planting in late winter, planted the crops in the spring or harvested the crops in late summer or sometimes fall. He usually worked from sunup to sunset in the fields for planting and harvesting with only a break for lunch. In the evening, he milked the cows again.

Matthew exhaled a deep breath. "I'm happy we have the beach and boating to look forward to, but I wish *Mamm* would be alive to go with us."

"Me too. I miss *Mamm*." Noah looked like he was ready to cry.

"Noah and I like it when we're in school because we can pretend *Mamm* is alive and busy in the kitchen."

Showing them the picture of *Mamm* which Aunt Carrie had given her was tempting... but that would be a poor substitute and probably wouldn't help at this point. "It's hard, I know. We are fortunate that we can share our feelings with each other. Adam's friend, Nick, recently lost his mother—"

"Did she have a heart attack too?" Noah asked.

She shook her head. "She died in a car accident. Nick doesn't have any brothers or sisters but we have each other. *Mamm* would want us to enjoy being with each other."

"Rachel, I'm glad you're home. I love you." Noah reached to grasp her hand, giving it a squeeze.

"*Ya*. The house was too lonely without you and *Mamm*."

"I love you both too." Her throat felt thick and her eyes filled with tears. "You know who *Mamm's* very best friend was?"

Noah thought for a minute. "Mrs. Maddox."

She shook her head. "Matthew, do you know?"

"It must be Samuel's *Mamm.*"

"You're wrong too, Matthew, but good answers. It's true *Mamm* loved her women friends. But she told me that her very best friend was Jesus. It says in the Bible that we can have contentment whatever the circumstances when we stay close to Jesus. Whenever you miss *Mamm*, pray to Jesus like she did every day. I know she misses all of us but I believe with my whole heart that she's happy to be with her best friend. Of course, you can still talk to me, *Daed*, Judith and Peter."

Matthew yawned while Noah said, "*Danki*, Rachel."

"You're welcome. Say your prayers now and get some sleep."

I'm glad Samuel understands how the twins need me to be in their lives on a daily basis yet. I want to marry him in the fall but maybe we should wait another year.

CHAPTER TWENTY

"My heart feels light now, Aunt Carrie." Rachel glanced at her *aenti*, driving. They were going to Weaver's Bakery to eat lunch and to celebrate. Bishop Amos had said Rachel could start her instructions to join the church. It was such a huge relief to be able to move on with her life and to continue her growth as a Christian.

"I'm glad I heard your good news in person before I go home."

She wanted to get her aunt's input about her *daed* re-marrying. The bishop had surprised her with his comments that she should encourage her father to remarry. Bishop Amos mentioned that his sister Barbara would be the ideal wife for her *daed*. The bishop felt strongly her *daed* should spend time soon with Barbara, so both could see if they suit each other enough to marry. "Bishop Amos seemed happy to see me, but I don't think it was all due to the fact I want to join the church. He was eager to talk to me about *Daed's* future wife. He told me that it was time for *Daed* to marry again."

Aunt Carrie frowned. "I don't think David's ready to even think about remarrying. He loved Irene deeply. It has to be hard after living with someone for a lot of years to consider getting married for a second time. I can't imagine myself falling in love again if something should happen to Scott. But life's so fragile and we don't know what God has planned for us."

While in Cocoa Beach, she'd overheard her uncle talk on the phone about running for president in the future. "Do you think Uncle Scott will run for president someday?"

"I hope he doesn't. He feels the stress enough from being a senator. He even mentioned getting out of politics, but the party wants him to consider seeking the nomination for president in the future." Aunt Carrie stopped at a red traffic light in Fields Corner. "I never dreamed we'd be in the public eye when we married. I thought we'd live a fairly quiet life. I knew it wouldn't be anything like an Amish lifestyle, but I never expected to have a husband in politics."

Once again she thought how her *aenti* never wore pants or the popular jeans like other English women wore. Today Aunt Carrie wore a black skirt and a long sleeved white blouse with a black cardigan. "If you'd known in the beginning that Uncle Scott wanted a political career, would you have made a different decision about getting married?"

"I honestly don't know. It might have scared me enough to back off for a time, but in the end, I think I would've still married him. It definitely hasn't been easy leaving the Amish community, but if I had married an Amish man I wouldn't have Adam and Violet."

I wonder how many children Samuel and I'll have. Would they have a large Amish family like many in their community did, or would they only be blessed with a small family? In their world, families usually ranged from eight to ten children. Amish couples never practiced birth control and prayed for children. "*Mamm* said a lot that *kinner* were such a blessing. She would have welcomed having more children. Samuel's *mamm's* disappointed that she only has three children."

Aunt Carrie nodded. "Children are a blessing from the Lord. Irene and I were blessed with great *kinner.* I would've liked more than two, but it wasn't God's will."

As the light turned green, she said, "We seem to spend a lot of time in the car together. I bet you're going to miss me when you drive back home."

"It'll be lonely without you riding with me. At least, Scott's coming home this evening so that will be nice. I won't be rattling around in the house by myself."

"I wonder if Mary Zook will wait on us."

"She has to know by now that she's not going to get Samuel away from you." Aunt Carrie glanced at her. "I bet Mary's cousin called and told her what Violet said about you and Samuel dating for two years and that he asked you to marry him."

"Mary doesn't give up easily."

"Is there going to be a fall wedding? I've been thinking about what we should get you for a wedding gift."

"I'm not positive but we're thinking about a November wedding." She grinned. "Don't say anything yet to anyone. Samuel hasn't asked *Daed* for my hand in marriage. Remember we are to keep our engagement a secret until late summer. Then Samuel and I can share it with our family." She liked how the Amish didn't bother with engagement rings and didn't announce an engagement until a few weeks ahead of the wedding ceremony. Samuel would be giving her an engagement gift instead of a ring. *I wonder if he'll give me the customary clock or a china set.*

"I'll keep your secret. We should get you a gas refrigerator and stove for your new house."

"That's too generous."

"Well, at least we can get one big kitchen appliance for you. You love to cook and bake so we'll get you a stove. I love cooking on a gas stove. "Aunt Carrie paused for a moment and continued, "Will Samuel have the house built in time? But I'm sure Peter and David will help build it plus Samuel's family. It'd be fun to have Scott and Adam help with your house too. They would need a lot of direction but they're quick learners."

"We're thinking about living with my family for several months so you don't have to buy the gas stove until we move. Samuel suggested it. He thinks it'll be better for my brothers."

"Samuel's a keeper. I hope someday Violet meets a nice and good man like Samuel."

"Violet's hoping Nick will become interested in her but you know that."

Aunt Carrie parked the SUV in the side lot next to the bakery. "She has liked Nick since he was a roommate with Adam their first year at college."

"I can't believe we got here so quickly. It takes much longer when I'm driving the buggy."

"Fields Corner's a lovely little town." Aunt Carrie glanced at the various businesses as she removed the key from the ignition. "How long has the fabric store been here?"

"Not too long. Maybe four months. It's been a blessing having it here so we don't have to go as far to get material for our clothes."

"Is it owned by an Amish woman?"

She nodded. "It's owned by two partners. One woman's Amish and one's English. They have yarn too."

"I'll stop in and get yarn for my shawls before I start home."

"You certainly are great at supporting Amish women and their businesses."

As soon as they entered the bakery, Katie led them to a round table next to a window.

"I'll take your order, then ask *Mamm* if I can join you for a few minutes. As you can see, we have few customers. We do have several to go orders that I need to help fill."

Aunt Carrie ordered a chicken pot pie and coffee. Rachel decided on the soup of the day which was potato soup. She added a toss salad and iced tea to her order.

Katie flipped the white cup on the table over and left with their orders, saying she'd be back soon with their drinks.

"Do you think they should put restaurant in the name?" Aunt Carrie asked. "Maybe they'd get more customers."

"Mrs. Weaver doesn't want to do that since they're mainly a bakery. She serves breakfast and lunch because there isn't any place else to eat in Fields Corner except a pizza place." Rachel grinned. "And she added the menu for meals when Samuel opened his furniture store. He likes to eat here for a break."

Katie set Rachel's glass of tea on the table before pouring coffee in Aunt Carrie's cup. Mrs. Weaver said hello to them as she brought a basket of warm whole wheat rolls and Rachel's salad. "I'm happy you're back home, Rachel. When Samuel told me you wanted to work here again, it made my day."

"*Danki*, for the rolls. They smell and look delicious." Aunt Carrie broke a roll apart before buttering it.

"It's good you two are here now because Katie can't wait to tell you about her new plan. I need to get back to the kitchen, but we'll talk more later." Mrs. Weaver smiled at them before she rushed away.

Katie pulled a chair away from the table and said, "While you two eat, I'll tell you what I have in mind."

Rachel dumped a little dressing on her salad. She liked her Thousand Island dressing on the side because too much prevented her from actually tasting the vegetables. "Why don't you eat with us?"

"I had a sandwich before you came in, but I'll eat dessert with you later." Katie scooted her chair in closer to the table. "I'm not going to wait around to see if I get married."

"Just because Tim wasn't for you, God might have someone else in mind to be your husband." She looked her friend over carefully and realized Katie seemed extremely happy about something.

"I know but if it doesn't happen, I can be an aunt to your children." Katie's blue eyes twinkled. "Of course, I hope children don't happen too soon because I need your help in my new business."

Aunt Carrie sipped her coffee. "I love it. Another new business in Fields Corner."

What could Katie possible have in mind? She'd already committed to working again at the bakery. With Judith studying for her GED exam, she couldn't devote herself to working at another place. "What do you have in mind?"

"I want to start a catering business. I'd like you to bake the cakes and cookies. I know you're going to work here again, so it can be on a trial basis. I'll have to arrange for an English driver to get me to places that might take too long by buggy. I want to do wedding receptions, school athletic banquets, and any type of anniversary parties."

"I wish I didn't live so far away. I'd definitely love you to cater some of the parties we give."

"Too bad you and your husband couldn't move to Fields Corner." Katie arched her eyebrow. "I'd get all kinds of business if I catered parties for a famous senator and his wife. Not that I should brag, though. That wouldn't be right. I'll stay humble even if I do well."

"What will you call your new business?" She jabbed her fork into a tomato, thinking how catering sounded like a lot of work but didn't want to discourage Katie. It was a relief to see her excited about something again.

"I'm thinking of Katie's Catering. So what do you think, Rachel?"

"I can bake cakes and help you get started. I'll have to see how it works out with taking care of my *daed* and brothers plus working here." Katie had talked for years about growing up so she could get married and have children. "Well, maybe you'll meet some nice Amish man while you do your catering."

Katie shrugged. "I doubt that. I'll probably be catering for the English get-togethers. I won't meet any Amish man. I don't care anymore about getting married. God might want me to remain single and serve others as a single woman. I can be more helpful to *Mamm* at home and still work in the bakery."

"Are you sure Tim's out of the picture? I can't see him leaving our church to marry an outsider."

"Even if Tim decides to stop seeing the English woman and wants to date me again, I'll refuse. I'm excited about having a cottage business. I guess it's in my blood already with two profitable businesses in the family."

Mrs. Weaver placed the chicken pot pie and a bowl of soup on the table. "Rachel, if you can start here on Tuesday, I'd appreciate it."

"I'll be here early on Tuesday. *Danki*, for hiring me part-time."

"Samuel asked me to tell you to stop in after you eat lunch." Mrs. Weaver touched her shoulder before glancing at Aunt Carrie. "I'll pray you have a safe trip home. I'm glad the weather's cooperating and it's not raining or snowing."

"Thank you." Aunt Carrie said in a sympathetic voice, "Martha, I'm sorry about your sister. You and your family are in my prayers. "

"It was a shock, that's for sure. It's hard on the children and my brother-in-law. And she left a newborn baby."

"Does your brother-in-law have anyone to help him?"

Mrs. Weaver nodded. "His own mother lives with them. It's a blessing he has her to help with the baby and other children."

While the two older women continued their conversation, Katie whispered to Rachel, "Samuel and I saw your newspaper pictures this morning. We didn't tell *Mamm* about them. Fortunately, Mary's been busy baking cupcakes for a baby shower so she was in the back when we saw the paper."

She hoped Samuel hadn't bought the newspaper so he could see her pictures. "I told him about them on Sunday. Is he upset about the one with Nick? It's not what it looks like."

"*Ya*, he's not happy about the headline and the pictures. A customer showed me the paper at the counter this morning because she recognized you. Samuel was here eating breakfast and he heard her asking me if you had left the Amish community." She gave an apologetic glance. "I had to show it to Samuel."

"It's okay. I'll go see him."

Katie stood. "I better scoot and get back to work."

* * *

Samuel couldn't get the picture of Rachel and Nick out of his mind. Hearing about it from Rachel was one thing but actually seeing Nick and Rachel together on the bench was something else. Tapping his fingers against his desk, he thought how people said that a picture was worth a thousand words. Not pleasant words in this case. *Why would Rachel sit right next to Nick in her skimpy clothes?* Sure, she said it was innocent and how they spoke about their mothers. She'd explained how the picture wasn't accurate because the bench was small and they had to sit close together. He'd liked the photo better if she had talked to Nick during the daytime in her Plain clothing. Then there wouldn't be a picture of them looking like they were enjoying a romantic night on the beach.

Their closeness on the bench obviously inspired the photographer to snap the photo and to submit it to the newspaper. He hated the headline, "A new love match between Senator Robinson's Amish niece and a family friend." Was Rachel telling the whole truth about her conversation with Nick? It looked like to him that Adam's friend was interested in Rachel. Would Nick have wanted to spend time with Rachel if she had been unpleasant to look at? Maybe that was being judgmental, but had Nick hoped to take advantage of Rachel's beauty and innocence? He sighed. Nick was Adam's friend so probably nothing happened to cause him to worry.

He definitely needed to talk to Rachel about this bench picture. Even the volleyball shot bothered him. She and her family might go to Outer Banks in the summer to visit with the Robinsons. Would Nick happen to pop up again so he could spend more time with Rachel?

He decided to make phone calls to his customers while Rachel ate lunch with her aunt. That would give him something constructive to do while he waited for Rachel. When he was on the fourth call, he heard Rachel come into the shop.

She pulled a chair next to his and smiled. He noticed how pretty she looked in a lavender dress. After Samuel finished his call, he asked, "How was lunch?"

"It was delicious." Sighing, she smoothed her apron. "It's *gut* Katie has something else to think about other than Tim, but I don't know about this catering business. She wants me to help her by baking cakes and cookies."

Katie must not have mentioned to Rachel that he saw the newspaper photos. He thought sure Katie would tell Rachel why he wanted to talk to her. "She wants the best baker. Did you bake while you were in Florida?"

She shook her head. "No. I cooked breakfast once for Violet and Aunt Carrie. I helped prepare the meals but never baked. Why do you ask?"

"I know how much you enjoy baking so I've wondered if you had any time to bake for your relatives. Or maybe make a special pie for someone?"

"Is Nick...the someone you have in mind?"

"*Ya.* It seems you were busy spending time walking and playing with Nick. Is that why you didn't have time to bake?"

CHAPTER TWENTY-ONE

Rachel raised her eyebrows at him. "Obviously, you saw the beach pictures. That's why I warned you about them on the phone. I didn't want you to take them the wrong way. There was no love match between me and Nick."

"The headline wasn't any better than the picture."

"No, it wasn't."

"The picture with you wearing your Plain clothing was nice. I liked it but I didn't like the other two photos."

What did he find offensive about the volleyball game picture? Was it because she had capris and a blouse on? "What was wrong with the picture of all of us playing volleyball?"

Samuel crossed his arms. "You had this big smile on your face when you looked at Nick."

"We were playing on the same team. What did you want me to do? Give him a nasty look?"

"Hearing you tell me about the bench picture was one thing, but actually seeing it is something else. You and Nick looked close and like you were involved with each other." He chewed on his bottom lip. "Nick saw more of you than I ever have. You were in a swimming suit and in skimpy clothes around him."

She stared at Samuel, wishing he'd never seen the newspaper pictures. Clearly, he hadn't been able to dismiss them as being just what they were...innocent pictures. Sullivan had made it look like a romance could be brewing between her and Nick. All she wanted was to get away to enjoy the ocean and a new environment in hopes she could resolve her negative feelings about her *daed* and make a decision whether to join the church or not. She had never been interested in meeting a young man in hopes of falling in love on the beach.

Folding her hands in her lap, she said in a gentle voice, "There was nothing at all between us. It was like I told you on the phone. We talked about our mothers and how it hurt losing them. Nick wasn't even in Cocoa Beach very long. He left on Saturday to spend time with his dad. I went on one walk with him. If I'd known that he wasn't going to watch a movie with Adam, I never would've gone swimming in the pool. As soon as he came out to the pool, I put Aunt Carrie's cover-up on before we walked on the beach." *Why was she explaining all this to Samuel? She never did anything wrong.*

"I don't think you should've walked with Nick by yourself. If Violet had gone with you, then the bench would've been too small for three people."

She exhaled a deep breath. "Violet wasn't available to walk with us. She was talking with her dad about her summer job. She's going to work for him so they had things to discuss."

"I'm sorry. I just was surprised to see the pictures." Samuel leaned closer to her. "I believe you."

Katie entered the store, looking worried. "Rachel, someone's in the bakery to see you."

Samuel smiled at her. "I bet a customer wants to know when you'll be helping with the baking again."

"He's not a customer," Katie said. "He's talking to your Aunt Carrie right now. She was pretty surprised to see him."

Could Nick be in Fields Corner? Who else could it be? Violet had overheard Nick asking for her address. Oh no, had Nick already gone to her house? Was this the time to tell Samuel that Nick had been interested in her, but she never gave him any encouragement? "Katie, did he give his name?"

Katie nodded. "Nick Foster. And it gets better. He flew here in his own plane."

Unhappiness flashed across Samuel's face. "Why would Nick fly to Fields Corner? Hey, we don't have an airport."

"He rented a car and drove from the airport. He's resourceful." Katie patted Samuel's arm. "Don't worry. Rachel loves you, big brother."

"Rachel, he has to either think he's already courting you or hopes to."

She smoothed her black apron, trying to think what to tell Samuel. Finally, her eyes met his. "I told you the truth. We talked about our mothers. Nick has to realize that my feelings for you are strong and deep. When he made me feel a bit uncomfortable, I wore my Plain clothing around him."

In a sharp voice, Samuel said, "I knew he did something. Did he kiss you?"

"No, but Nick looked at me once like he wanted to. And he talked about visiting me this summer, but I hoped he wouldn't. After he left Cocoa Beach, Violet told me that Nick had asked Adam for my address, but I didn't think he'd come here when I never gave him any encouragement. Adam also told him that I was serious about you."

Katie briefly touched her hand. "I'll tell him whatever you want me to."

"I wish he'd go away but I better see him and get it over with. *Danki* for warning me that he's here." She looked at Samuel and hated seeing the hurt in his blue eyes. She couldn't tell him about Nick's tweet. Samuel might think she wasn't telling the truth about how nothing had happened at Cocoa Beach. It seemed hard to believe that Nick barely knew her, but yet he tweeted how he met the girl he wanted to marry.

Then Nick flew to Ohio to see her. There wasn't an airport in Fields Corner, so that meant he went to a lot of trouble to see her. How could he think he had a chance with her? Real love didn't happen like that. Why did he have to come and spoil a *wunderbaar* day? She'd be firm and tell him that he needed to focus on meeting someone from his world.

As they left Samuel, Katie said, "I can't keep a man and you have two. But I don't envy you. I don't think Nick's going to leave right away. What are you going to do?"

"Tim's a fool and he might realize he made a mistake." She walked beside Katie on the sidewalk. "I'm sure Nick will leave soon. He doesn't have any place to stay tonight."

"He could book a room at Miller's bed and breakfast."

"Katie, don't you dare tell him about it. I'm hoping he doesn't realize there's a place he can spend the night."

She took a deep breath as Katie opened the front door of the bakery for her. Nick sat at the table with Aunt Carrie. He saw her instantly and waved to her. No doubt about it, Nick Foster was a handsome man with charisma. Actually now that she thought about it, his personality seemed a little like her uncle's. Too bad Nick couldn't be interested in Violet. They'd make a cute couple. When she saw how his eyes filled with eagerness and hope at her arrival, she became worried. *She prayed silently, Please help me to make Nick realize that I will never be interested in him without hurting his feelings.*

"Rachel, I was just telling Carrie how beautiful the countryside is here. I like the way everything looks without electrical wires. All the farms with their large white houses are amazing. I stopped before I got here to see a greenhouse business. Mr. Miller showed me the diesel engine he uses to run his greenhouse business."

Oh no, that meant Nick saw the Miller's bed and breakfast. Shouldn't he be going back to college, she thought. "When does your college start again?"

"I'm going to fly back tonight. I just wanted to see you before my classes start." He flashed her a big grin. "Unless you'd like me to stay tonight. Mr. Miller told me there was an available room at the Blue Ridge Inn."

"Excuse me, but I want to get yarn for my shawls before I start back home." Aunt Carrie stood and said to Rachel, "I'll come back and drive you home."

Before she got a chance to thank her aunt, Nick said, "I can take Rachel home."

Aunt Carrie laughed. "That's not a good idea. Amish don't believe in fighting but Samuel might decide to make an exception if he sees Rachel in your car."

"*Danki*, Aunt Carrie." She wasn't just thanking her aunt for the ride home, but for trying to get in Nick's thick skull that Samuel might feel like fighting for her.

Katie stopped by their table and asked, "Would you like more coffee?"

"Yes, please." After Nick thanked Katie, he said, "Your town and surrounding area is beautiful with all the farms. It's such a relaxing and peaceful atmosphere that I feel like telling Mr. Robinson I can't work for him this summer. I could instead work on my thesis for my Master's here."

"I'll be right back." She picked up her glass to get more iced tea. She needed to think what she should say to Nick. While she watched her glass fill with liquid, it hit her that Nick became interested in her to get past the sadness in his life. By his instant romantic interest, he was grasping for someone to get him out of the deep well of grief he'd been experiencing from losing his mother. Having her in his life gave him something new to think about so his pain would lessen a bit. When he felt a need to talk about his mother, Nick felt comfortable talking to her. She was one person who could relate to his pain and knew what it was exactly like to lose a beloved mother.

She pushed on the spigot to stop the tea flow. *Nick seems to like that I'm Amish. I think that's another reason he's attracted to me... something unique. I definitely don't want him coming this summer to work on his thesis.*

On her way back to the table, Katie whispered, "He's all yours. Good luck."

Before sitting, she asked, "Why did you want to see me? I'm surprised you would fly here."

"I told you I'd visit you. You didn't tell me not to."

"That would've been rude." She gave him a little smile. "I love Samuel and you being here is hard to explain to him when I don't know why you're here."

"I'm fallen in love with you."

"You barely know me."

"My Dad fell in love with my mother at first sight so it can happen." Nick leaned forward in his chair. "Maybe you were meant to meet me. You left Fields Corner to experience new things because you've lived a sheltered life. I bet Samuel's the only guy you've ever dated."

It wasn't Nick's business if Samuel was the only one she'd dated. "I'm sorry, but I'm not going to fall in love with you."

He grinned. "Don't be so sure about that. I've been told I can be downright irresistible to women."

"I talked to Bishop Amos about joining our church this morning. I'm going to start taking instructions and will be baptized. Then I'll be able to marry Samuel."

He looked at her hands. "I don't see any engagement ring on your finger."

"Amish women don't wear jewelry. Engagement and wedding rings are not exchanged by Amish couples."

"Your aunt didn't marry an Amish man."

"Aunt Carrie had to be deep in love to leave the world she grew up in. It's good she has always had such a strong love for my Uncle Scott because I don't think they would've made it otherwise."

"Are you positive you want to be Amish and marry Samuel? You're young yet and might change your mind later." His eyes bored into hers. "While we were on the beach, you didn't protest about me visiting you here."

"I didn't want to hurt your feelings, but I didn't exactly encourage you to visit either. I want to be Amish and to marry Samuel. He's bought land for us so we can build a house on it." Should she mention Violet to him? If he'd be interested in her cousin, that would be wonderful. Violet would be happy and she could see those two as a couple. No, probably not a good idea to bring up Violet. Nick might jump to the wrong conclusion and think that was why she wasn't interested in him. He'd feel she wanted to avoid hurting her cousin. "It was good for us to express our feelings to each other about our mothers.

It helped me to vent to you. And I hope it helped you to talk to me about your mother."

He nodded. "You said that on the beach how maybe we met for that reason only. I want more. I want you in my life, Rachel."

"I'm sorry but what you want isn't possible. It's time for us to move on with our lives. Our mothers would want us to be happy. I'm looking forward to becoming Mrs. Samuel Weaver. You have a lot in your life to focus on. And maybe you'll meet someone special this summer while you work for my Uncle Scott."

He shook his head. "I won't forget you that fast. If I lived in your world and became Amish, would I have a chance with you?"

"It's hard for an outsider to become Amish. Our world is so different. I can't see you driving a buggy and going without electricity."

"For some reason, I can't see you in my world either. You belong here. I can see that now."

His sad expression spoke volumes to her. *Where was Aunt Carrie? How much yarn was she buying?* "When I left Fields Corner, I thought about not joining the church. After praying on the beach and living briefly in the English world, I realized I wanted to always be Amish. This is my home where I can best serve God."

"I think I knew this was going to be a wasted trip but I wanted to see you again. Even though I haven't been successful in convincing you to give me a chance, it hasn't been a wasted trip. I've enjoyed talking with you."

"I wish you'd called first. You could've saved yourself some time and money."

"How could I call when you don't have a phone?"

"You could've called my aunt's cell phone. But we do have a phone now. My father put a phone in while I was at the beach. It's in small building outside our house."

"Hey, that's progress." He drank his coffee. "I'd like to meet your family."

She glanced at her watch. "School will let out soon. How about you meet Judith and my brothers here in town before you leave?"

"Sure. That sounds good." He winked at her. "What about Samuel? I'd like to meet him and tell him how lucky he is."

She grinned. "He already knows that."

CHAPTER TWENTY-TWO

On the way home, Rachel decided to tease her *aenti*. "I should've offered to drive on these back roads."

"You must be feeling better to joke about driving."

"It seemed you were gone a long time at the quilt shop, but it turned out okay. I probably needed the extra time to talk to Nick. I just worried a bit that Samuel would ask Katie how long we chatted."

"Samuel knows enough to trust you." Aunt Carrie glanced at her. "I enjoyed my conversation with Sarah. If your *daed* ever decides to remarry and I'm not saying he should... but Sarah might be someone he should consider. She's sweet and is a widow, but you probably know that."

She frowned. "I never even gave Sarah a thought. Her daughter, Abigail, is the same age as Noah and Matthew. Judith enjoys having her in class. Sarah isn't in our church district so *Daed* has never met Sarah."

"Well, if it's meant to be, David will remarry sometime. I know he's not anxious to date Barbara. I took a big liking to Sarah immediately."

"Did you meet her English co-owner, Laura? She's nice too."

Aunt Carrie shook her head. "No. She wasn't around."

"I can't see *Daed* with anyone else but *Mamm*, but I do like Sarah. Maybe I can invite her and Abigail to supper sometime." They were almost to the Hershberger farm, and she hated to see Aunt Carrie leave. "I'm going to miss you. *Danki*, for everything. I had a *wunderbaar* time at your house and on the beach with everyone."

"I'll miss you too. I can't wait until summer when we get together at Outer Banks. Don't worry. I'll make sure we keep it quiet so there will be no photographers. I'll tell Adam not to bring Nick either."

"Maybe Nick will see Violet as someone he can date instead of just looking at her as Adam's younger sister." Meeting Nick had helped her work through feelings of grief. "It was constructive to vent our grief to each other."

As she turned into their driveway, Aunt Carrie said, "I enjoyed your visit a lot. I'm glad you have a phone so we can stay in touch. We can talk a couple of times a month."

She nodded. "I like that."

* * *

Rachel wasn't surprised when her brothers yelled from the porch, "Samuel's here." She knew he'd stop by after closing the store.

Judith laughed. "We definitely don't need a doorbell with those two boys around. Nothing or anyone gets past them."

"He's checking to see if Nick's here."

"Why would Samuel think Nick's here? You said he left Fields Corner."

"Nick left with me to meet you, Noah, and Matthew, so Samuel might think we invited him here. I made sure Katie knew why I left with Nick so she'd tell Samuel." She shrugged. "But obviously Samuel's checking to see if Nick has really left."

"Or he just wants to spend time with you." Judith grinned. "He knows you love him. You came back. You didn't run after Nick."

She removed a butterscotch pie from the gas refrigerator and placed it on the kitchen counter.

Judith smiled. "You whipped up that pie fast."

"I had time since you already had a casserole in the oven for supper."

Judith' smile widened in approval. "I can see why you made Samuel's favorite dessert. It should help to lighten his mood."

She nodded. "I hope so. I don't think you have to worry about your cooking skills any longer. Sometime we'll work on desserts and I'll give you some pie-making tips."

"I can now cook two recipes without ruining them. I have a lot to learn yet."

"We should make a yummy dessert together so you have something to take to the Sunday sing."

Noah opened the kitchen door with Samuel behind him. "Your boyfriend's here, Rachel."

Judith gave Noah a push. "Let's go in the living room and let these two chat. Where's Matthew?"

"He went to the barn to see *Daed*."

Over his shoulder, Noah said, "I can't wait until you marry Rachel."

Samuel arched his eyebrows. "Why's that?"

"Because it'll be fun to have another guy around here. We don't see Peter enough since he got married. Judith said you'll live here until your house is built."

"I hope so." After Judith and Noah had left, Samuel gave her a mischievous look. "Do I get a piece or are you going to throw the pie at me instead?"

She put her hands on her hips. "That depends. Did you come for my pie or to see if I'm hiding Nick?"

"I know Nick's not here." Samuel took her hand in his big one. "If things would have been reversed and a photographer had taken pictures of me with a beautiful English woman on the beach, wouldn't you have questioned me about what had happened?"

"I suppose so. Especially if she'd came to Fields Corner to see you like Nick did." She rolled her eyes at him. "What about Mary Zook? She's Amish and she's certainly been after you while I've been gone."

Samuel laughed. "It's good you're back to save me from Mary's clutches."

I better make sure Samuel knows Nick understands that he doesn't have a chance with me. "I made it clear to Nick that nothing will ever happen between us. I told him again how I love you. And I never led him on at all on the beach."

"I wish I could've been the one to help you move on with your life. It was hard to hear another man was the one to help you with your grief. That was selfish of me."

"Oh, Samuel. You've always been my rock. Your constant prayers for me were helpful. And God was with me here in Fields Corner, but on the beach I was able to feel His presence and love even more."

"I'm glad you had a break from your daily routine. It was a blessing."

She felt fully alive with happiness and squeezed Samuel's hand.

"I can see why Nick fell for you. You're a beautiful woman. Not just on the outside but on the inside too." He pulled her into his arms. "Rachel, I love you."

She felt the strength in his muscled arms. Even though, he worked hours on building furniture, helping his *daed* and *bruder* on the farm kept his body toned. His touch sent warmth through her body.

He bent down and kissed her for an unbelievably long moment. His wonderful kiss felt like a warm summer breeze that is perfect in every way.

"That was some kiss." She gazed into his blue eyes. "I love you, Samuel. I can't wait until we marry and have lots of *bopplin*."

"How about a November wedding?"

"That sounds perfect." She touched his chin. "I'm trying to picture you with a beard."

He brushed his lips against her forehead. "We'll have a *gut* life."

"Would you like a piece of pie now?"

"The pie can wait. I want to kiss you again before your family pops in here."

As his warm lips met hers, she had only one thought. God had blessed her greatly. She'd grown up in a *wunderbaar*, Christian family and now she gave thanks to Him for her Samuel.

My inspiration for writing this book came from my sweet late mother, Laoma Oberly Wilson. She lived a long Christian life and enjoyed being a wife, mother and grandmother. Her grandfather was a Mennonite minister, and she shared many stories about him. Even though she wasn't Amish and later wasn't Mennonite, she kept many of their Christian beliefs while attending a Protestant church. I'm sharing a favorite family cookie recipe of hers. I hope you enjoy my mother's thumbprint cookie recipe.

THUMBPRINT COOKIE RECIPE

Ingredients

1 cup soft shortening

½ c. brown sugar packed

2 egg yolks

1 tsp. vanilla

2 cups flour

½ tsp. salt

2 egg whites

¾ c. nuts

Directions

Preheat oven to 350 degrees.

Mix shortening, brown sugar, egg yolks and vanilla. Mix together flour and salt. Stir in other ingredients.

Roll 1 tsp. dough into ball. Dip in slightly beaten egg white. Roll in nuts and put on baking sheet.

Press thumb in center of each cookie.

Bake 10 to 12 minutes. Cool. You can put confectionary frosting or candied fruit in center. My mother always put white frosting in the center.

ABOUT THE AUTHOR

As the youngest in the family, growing up on a farm in Findlay, Ohio, Diane often acted out characters from her own stories in the backyard. In high school she was the student sitting in class with a novel hidden in front of her propped up textbook. Her passion for reading novels had to be put on hold during her college years at Ohio State University due to working part-time on campus and being a full-time student.

Before starting on her writing career, Diane was a school teacher and play director. She enjoys her life with her husband, six children, daughter-in-law, son-in-law and four grandchildren in southwestern Ohio. Her husband and children are very supportive of her writing.

She writes Amish fiction, contemporary romance, Christian romance, historical fiction, women's fiction and chick-lit mystery.

OTHER BOOKS BY DIANE CRAVER

Amish Fiction
Judith's Place, Dreams of Plain Daughters, Book 2
Fleeting Hope, Dreams of Plain Daughters, Book 3
A Decision of Faith, Dreams of Plain Daughters, Book 4

Amish Shorter Works
An Amish Starry Christmas Night, Book 1
An Amish Starry Summer Night, Book 2

Inspirational Romance
When Love Happens Again
Marrying Mallory

Chick-Lit Mystery
A Fiery Secret

Contemporary Romance
Whitney in Charge
Never the Same
The Proposal – as a short and also in A Christmas
    Collection: Anthology
Yours or Mine

Historical Fiction and Inspirational
A Gift Forever

VISIT DIANE ONLINE!

Website and Blog:

www.dianecraver.com

www.dianecraver.com/blog

Facebook:

www.facebook.com/#!/pages/
Diane-Craver/153906208887

Made in the USA
Middletown, DE
19 January 2016